Journey to a Darker World

By Christian Mathis

Special thank you to Brandon Croft for listening to hundreds of bad ideas, while still helping me come up with great ones.

Prologue

Collins

THUD. THUD. THUD. The door shook and cracked, finally bursting open with a shudder as the armies of the new world converged at the stronghold. They had one common goal, capturing the man with the death touch, the most dangerous man in the world.

"Colonel Collins, the threat is located on the upper level, how should we proceed?" Voice shaking with excitement and a touch of fear, the soldier stood ready to execute my orders.

"Capture him alive if you can, the President wants to have him questioned." The soldier saluted and assembled his troops to begin the raid. Filing in, checking the room, their footsteps rang through the night.

An agent near me opened a closet. None of us saw the hand reach down to grab his shoulder; he was dead before he hit the floor, body pumped full of cobra venom. Unseen, Catalyst shifted through the shadows, attacking one man after another. A single touch and a trace amount of Bufo toad poison froze a nervous system. Each man received a different poison as if Catalyst were casually toying with them, honing his skills.

I caught a glimpse of him as he crept down the stairs, his athletic silhouette briefly framed in the doorway before he entered the next room. Drawing my gun, I went to the doorway and did a quick look into the room. His red eyes shone across the room, and I blindly squeezed off e round in my gun, finally hearing the thump as his body hit the floor, a heavy dose of tranquilizers coursing through his veins.

Hours later, I slammed shut the door of his specially made tempered glass cell. I had a meeting to get to; it was an important day. For the first time, I was allowed to be a member of the Council. An elite group of former presidents, royalty, and important political and military leaders. The members each led a coalition reporting directly to the leader of the United Nations, Director Alvarez. It was the first meeting after the Restructuring. The world had been divided into five regions; old boundaries were erased and replaced by the North American Coalition, South American Coalition, African Coalition, Europe-Asia Coalition, and the Australian -Arctic Coalition. I took my seat in time for the meeting to start.

The President of the North American Coalition slammed his hands on the metal conference table in frustration. The room grew quiet as everyone took their seats. The Council was gathered in Union City to discuss recent global chaos and how...if...it could be corrected.

"The super-powered extremists must be dealt with before they can rally others to their cause. After the attack on the New Africa Coalition that killed thousands, we need to know what prison can hold them immediately." The President's cold, black eyes roved the room. Voices rose as delegates began shouting over one another.

"Let us build a prison that can hold them."

"Let's set them out to sea; fate will decide what will become of them."

"If we cannot imprison them then we must kill them "

"I work aboard the shield space station, and we recently discovered a planet which could be habitable." A clear voice cut across the yelling delegate, and all eyes turned to a woman sitting in the corner, awkwardly picking stuffing from a small hole in her chair. "I suggest we kill two birds with one stone and send the terrorists there. We get to see if the planet will sustain human life and get rid of the prisoners at the same time." She shrugged with a small smile, "Either way, it benefits us; if they live, we know it's a potential colony world. If they don't? Well...then they're dead."

A low buzzing sound began to emanate from my chair, low in pitch; it was like the ancient microwaves. I felt my chair start to turn around and face the voting screen. The board had 200 colored squares on it, one at a time they would change either black or gold. Black meant nay, and gold meant yea. I glanced down at the arm of my chair at the two glowing buttons. I ran my fingers through my dark, feeling the severity of my decision. With trembling fingers, I pushed the gold button and sealed the criminals' fate.

Thunderous applause roared through the building as the watching masses saw the voting screen lit up almost unanimously golden.

An image appeared on the screen of the new planet; it showed against the dark sky as shiny as a brand-new marble. The color was a mix between a dark silver and the chrome color of a ball bearing. A voice emanated from the speakers "This planet appears to be uninhabited by sentient life flourishes in vegetation. Located three light-years beyond the edges of the Milky Way. A ship should be able to reach it in a matter of days with the new prototype the "*Mach Infinity*." The computer voice clicked off with a ping

"Any questions concerning the mission or planet, "asked the director.

"Any questions?" asked the Director. "Yes, Col. Collins?" I ran my tongue over-dried lips so that I could speak clearly.

"What do we know about the terrorists and their powers?" The computer began to buzz, and rumble, images began to flash on the screen.

Name: Catalyst aka none

Hair: black

Eyes: grey, dark red when powers are used.

Height: 5’10”

Country of origin: North America Coalition

Abilities: poison creation can create any poison or toxin from any animal. Usually, it can only pass poison through touch and can also throw disease spores through the air.

Name: Raymond Clifford, aka Kinetic

Hair: Blond

Height 5’0”

Eyes: blue

Country of origin: Europe -Asia Coalition

Ability: energy conversion, kinetic to potential from any source

Name: James Whitlock aka Blood clot

Hair: none

Height: 6’8”

Eyes: brown

Country of origin: African coalition

Ability: utilizes the trace amounts of iron in his blood to create weapons, can cause his blood to coagulate, not effective on any other blood source

Name: Tonihvio Velasquez aka Warlord

Height: 5'11

Eyes: dark brown

Country of origin: South American coalition

Ability: complete photogenic recall of e battle or skirmish ever fought in human history.

Name: Annabel Bishop

Height: 5'6"

Hair: dark blonde

Eyes: brown

Country of origin: North American coalition

Abilities: unknown

The screen dimmed and shut off; the director stood up and spoke. "We will start finalizing plans first thing in the morning

A week had passed, the Mach Infinity was undergoing final trials, and as I passed the hangar towards the cell block, I heard the NAC President's voice.

"It's a new planet, rich in resources and minerals. We don't know if it's inhabited or safe for humans; with your extra abilities you can establish the first contact." His voice was oily, trying too hard to be convincing. "You could be true heroes.

Catalyst looked at him, angry and agitated.

"The only way we do this if we all get full pardons and we get to be left alone when we return."

The President gave a sly smirk.

"Deal, you will all be forgiven of your crimes on your return to earth "

I watched in anticipation; my fingers drummed against the hot metal bleachers. Catalyst and the rest of the crew climbed aboard the *Mach infinity*. The pitch-black spaceship was a prototype; it was a super-advanced remodel of the space shuttle the major difference Was the rocket boosters were built into the hull. It was able to shoot off like a rocket once in the atmosphere wings would release from the sides, and it would resemble a giant jet with supersonic engines were fast enough to jump light-years in a matter of hours.

The ship's door closed, and all personnel vacated the platform and runway. The heat of the massive engines burned against my skin. They began to lift off the ship bellowing noise loud and strong enough to shake the bleachers I sat on the flames burning a bright green and purple, I felt the ground shaking like an earthquake. The sky lit up with a blinding hot red light, and with a blink it was gone, and everything went quiet. The convicts barreled toward the distant planet at over four hundred times the speed of light.

Chapter One

"CATALYST, WAKE UP! James shook me awake. "Dude, I think we should check out the rest of the ship before we get to the planet," said James.

"Yeah, that is probably a good idea, man." I scanned the room took in my surroundings, besides James the mountain-sized man. All around the sleeping quarters, people were stirring. We'd been told before the launch that it was natural to pass out from the shock of traveling at such an incredible speed. They hadn't bothered to tell us that it would leave us feeling drunk and disoriented. I dashed across the room and caught him before his head hit the table. The first thing I noticed about him was his long sandy blonde hair, thin face and blue eyes that could light a room.

Raymond was still out of it, and when he spoke, his speech was slurred, and his eyes struggled to stay in one place. "Hey fuck off dude, Don't act like you did a lot, I would have fallen two feet. I will try not to get in the way of you patting yourself on the back. The name is Raymond; my friends call me Ray. So, you can call me Raymond.

I paused before I answered him, "My name is Catalyst because of what I can do. I don't go by my real name anymore."

Raymond stroked his hand over his chin before speaking, "what exactly can you do?"

"I can create toxins or venoms, usually only animal poisons like snakes or spiders, any animal which can poison I can mimic its poison, most times I have to be touching the person to poison them. Although recently I discovered I could throw disease spores from a distance."

Ray looked startled," Damn man, how many people did you kill before you could control your powers."

I paused before answering, "176 people died before I could control the amount of poison I administer."

"Well on that ominous note, I am Annabelle, I don't really have any Powers I think the president of the NAC sent me away because I was building a Militia, we were going to start a revolution," A feminine voice said from the corner.

She sauntered over to me, a smirk on her lips. Flipping long blonde hair over her shoulder, her grey eyes stared up at me through long lashes. I got the feeling she was much more dangerous than she was letting on.

"James grunted the man who had woken me, standing and stretching, we all watched the muscles roll along his massive arms." I can coagulate blood. Mine, specifically. Turn it into weapons."

Rip, crack. The tall man with bronze-colored skin, long dark hair and a pointed goatee had ripped his seat open and taken the metal support bars out, as he spoke, he attempted to sharpen it into a weapon.

"The name is Tonihio Velasquez; you can call me Toni, I have uncanny recall of any battle or war in history, ever tactic, ever strategy, outcome, first-person accounts as if I was there myself."

James started to wholeheartedly laugh, "Bro that's not a power. That's what history books are for."

Whoosh, thunk, a makeshift blade whizzed through and wedged itself deep into the wall inches behind James' right ear.

"Alright you can throw a knife, can you fight, he dislodged the knife and made a small deep cut on his left arm, blood dripped into his right hand. it hardened into a dagger, and James shot it through the air towards Toni's head.

BOOM, BOOM, suddenly, I was picked up and slammed into the wall, the ship turned and flipped and became inverted as we entered the foreign atmosphere, an incredibly loud series of pops as we slowed from light speed to the speed of sound.

The ship hit the ground with a heavy *thud* and bounced back up. The crew got tossed around like weightless rag dolls. The ship dragged along the ground with back-breaking jerking and shaking, we screeched to a halt. We stopped, and the silence burned in my ear.

"Uhh Uhh, a voice moaned from the darkness."

I managed to pull myself up to my knees and see who was moaning.

"Damn Toni, are you ok?"

He had a deep gouge in his forearm and blood ran down his arm and dripped to the floor, I took a seat cover off and wrapped it around his arm, then pulled it tight. I scanned the cabin to see if anyone else was Hurt.

"AHHHHHHH WHAT THE HELL!!!"

Ray screamed, I looked down on the floor and saw Ray's detached bloody finger on the floor of the cabin. His blood spurted on to the floor. Anabelle let out a loud huff.

"Uh damn man, you don't have to cry like a bitch; it will be alright. I once knew a guy with only two fingers on each hand."

I waited for a response from Ray, except one did not come. He was entranced with his stump.

James hurried over and placed his hand over Raymond's wounded hands. After a few moments, he pulled his hands away, the stumps of Ray's fingers had been cauterized through James mixed his blood and coagulating Rays.

"See, my powers don't suck. I cannot heal; recently I learned I could stop the bleeding by hardening the blood."

"Well now that the mayhem is done maybe we should check out the ship and see if the government gave us any supplies, besides we have an entire planet to explore "

"Why the hell would we leave the ship? The ship crashed on this planet. All we know about it is what they have told us. Which is probably only lies. We need to stay on the ship as long as we can before some giant ass bug or something eat us," said Toni.

I stroked my chin, "Toni, I get what you're saying, and I respect your military knowledge, I think we should take our supplies and explore. After all, the whole reason we were sent here was to see if the planet was habitable."

Ray ran his finger over the hardened blood on his hand. "Who put you in charge, dark and gruesome?"

Annabelle pulled herself onto the control panel and sat down. She ran her fingers along her scalp and pulled out a small metal file that was hidden in her hair before tossing it to Toni.

"the only way to decide who should lead is to vote."

"Or we could fight, to the victor go the spoils," said Toni.

My hands slid past each other, and I brought my index fingers to my lips. "Toni, I promise if we fight the only thing that will be spoiling is your corpse."

"Damn dude, I think we should follow Catalyst, not before grabbing the supplies," said James. The ship had narrow hallways; we were forced to walk in a straight line. Everyone spent more time checking on the others with a sideway glance then walking. When we reached the storage hold; dozens of crates lined the wall. *Crack.*

"What the fuck is this. What the actual hell IS THIS!" said James. He shattered a crate against the wall. The only thing that was left was a scrap of paper. On it was only one word. GOTCHA.

Toni picked up an empty crate and hurled it at my head.

"So much for your deal with the President, the son of a bitch banished us, exiled us, and sent us to die."

I thought about how stupid we had all been; they didn't want us to be heroes, they wanted us to get here and die or live and not be able to come back, I knew I had to stay positive. Maybe we could do it, live on this God-forsaken planet, or better yet get off.

Ray and Toni looked furious when they spoke hard and angry.

Raymond walked over to me and shoved me, knocking me back and onto the floor.

"This is all your fault! You agreed to come along. You're a bad guy. I'm the bad guy. We're all criminals, and you thought we could be heroes. IT'S YOUR FAULT WE'RE STUCK HERE!"

He took a swing at me and hit me square in the jaw. A small amount of blood trickled down my face. I wiped it off with my fingers.

"Look I'm sorry you think I got us stuck here if I hadn't agreed to go, we would have been forced anyway, I will do everything I can to get us home."

I had not seen Toni slip behind me, and he punched me in the side, I felt the hit in my kidney, I fell to my knees. I grabbed Toni's forearm and gave him a dose of the blue-capped ifrit a bird whose poison causes numbness, and he fell to the ground. The poison would turn his whole body numb as if a painful pins and needles were on every inch of his body

James stepped forward, clenched his fist, and screamed, "Now that is enough, we are not going to fight anymore!"

We searched the room for an hour, and the only thing we found was a few apples and a five-gallon jug of water. We held out for a week and then were forced to leave when we ran out of supplies.

The crew gathered around the outer door; we pulled on our suits, which were specially made for deep space journey capable of withstanding immense pressure and infused with an oxygen rebreather so that we could venture far from the ship without dying.

"What if there are people or creatures out there what will we use for weapons, we all can't make weapons from thin air like Sampson over here?" asked Ray. He still held his hand where his fingers used to be, stroking his chin as he always does.

Sssssssssshhhhhh "With these," Toni Said, dragging makeshift blades from things from the cabin, a sword from a chair arm, daggers from a crate.

"This one's for your big bro,"

He slid a homemade mace to James, made from a rod from an arm handle, and giant nails and screws formed the spikes.

Cuuwaaaaaswoosh the massive door opened, letting out the stale cabin air with a burst of steam, we shuffled forward, and I was the first down the steep steps. I was hesitant when I stepped off the stairs and onto the planet's surface, my footprint kicked up a cloud of black soot after everyone had stepped onto the ground.

"This is incredible," I said.

Everything was in grey, black, and white as if everything was living dead. Unlike Earth where certain colors are absorbed, and others refracted like the sky of Earth being refracted of blue, the shortest wavelength on this planet ever color must be absorbed, which leaves only black and grey," I said.

Annabelle reached down and plucked a strange-looking flower from the ash-colored ground; a plume of black soot filled the air. The flower was black with a spherical center with eight points jutting out. Suddenly, the flower exploded, and the razor-sharp points shot through the air and embedded into her oxygen rebreather.

I screamed, "Annabelle! Your suit!"

The hiss of the oxygen escaping her tank scared me even though I had just met her. The hissing stopped; her eyes jutted open.

"I don't need your help put me down!"

"The air must be breathable; we should be able to venture farther from the ship if we have to then,"

In all the chaos, we had not noticed a gurgling sound coming from the ship. Toni kneeled and dragged his fingers through the dirt, pulling his fingers to his face and examined the liquid.

"It is our fuel, look at the tank it's basically gone, THAT ROCK IS ALL THE WAY THROUGH THE GAS TANK WHAT THE HELL ARE WE GOING TO DO,"

"Guys, they may have sent us here to doom us, banish us, keep us from the fight, we will not be beat , we will find fuel or a ship, we will return to earth ,and we will defeat the crooked President and restore order and peace throughout the world most of all we will make him pay agonizingly for sending us to die , now let's explore this planet. Who's with me?"

"LET'S GO"

"What a stupid speech, don't act like you give some rousing, heroic speech. Most of us are merely following you because it is, the only option. Leave the ship or die," said James.

"There is no better motivation then mutual hatred and despise for everyone, I am in no matter what I got all of your backs," Said James."

We all grabbed our handcrafted blades pointed them in the middle and with clash raised them to the sky, and we knew we were united until the end."

We had started to walk again when the ground was losing and shifted with each step, which sent up clouds of dust and debris. I took one more step, and the entire ground gave away. I slipped under the earth, and I felt cold hard earth surround me, the ground pressed on my back and chest as if trying to squash me while it dragged me down at the same time, deeper and deeper. I slipped into the foreign dirt up to my neck as I felt it start to seep into my ears. I screamed and screamed.

I felt arms around James and me and Toni we're pulling me up once I was free, I had to pull the black sand out of my ears and everywhere else. "We're going to have to be careful moving on. There are pockets of ground that aren't solid.

Toni shouted, "I have an idea in World War II, a battle was fought in Anzio, Italy that pushed the Americans into the countryside where a mind field laid. One of the officers chucked rocks to see where it was safe to step; if they landed safely, it was ok to walk on them, and it blew up; they would have been dead to care. Let us do it until we get out of this valley, at least."

I fell back to the rear, and Toni took point. The others fell in the middle. I grabbed a piece of rubble from the ship, and I passed it to Annabel who passed it to James all the way down the line to Toni, he threw it, and it landed and immediately started to sink, I passed another piece and Toni threw it, and this time it landed flat and Toni took a step forward . We grabbed another piece of rubble, and assembly lined it down until we had created an entire pathway through the valley of darkness. Step. Step. Step one at a time, we all hopped over the last metal chunk.

"Guys, I'm tired we need to take a break, maybe camp for the night," said Annabel. I looked around at everyone's faces, and everyone looked exhausted and beat.

"I think you're right, we need rest," I said. Wssssshhhhwhhsh, a wind picked up instead of a cool breeze wind cut deep into our skin, like a thousand razor blades digging into your skin all at once. "Ahhh holy crap! Dammit! "Raymond screamed and ran forward."

He stumbled and fell into a hole like structured; it was a small cave. I said, "we can crawl inside and keep out of the razor wind."

The cave was cramped and crowded as we all pushed close together to get inside.

Plink Plink plink, I heard a slow dripping of water hitting the floor; it was almost black dark purple. "Bro you think that's safe to drink I'm thirsty," asked James.

"Maybe we should test somehow first," said Toni

James scooted over and stuck his tongue out close to the ceiling, and the water rolled down his tongue.

He fell sideways over and slumped to the floor.

"JAMES! what the hell, no!" I screamed

"Bahahaha, its fine, dude. I'm joking," James laughed his deep bellied laugh.

"Man, that's not funny we thought you died," said Toni

"Guys, let's get some sleep," I said as I lay down.

I felt the cold stone floor under my back when I drifted off to sleep.

I awoke with a jolt when I thought I heard whispers, alas, it was my dreams. I looked down, and I saw Annabel lying on my chest. The thin light accentuating the lines of her beautiful face, I wrapped my arms around her and fell back asleep.

"Who are they"

"Where did they come from."

"What are we going to do with them?"

I heard the whispers again, and my eyes popped open, and I glanced around the room.

I made eye contact with James

"Uh, catalyst," James said.

I felt someone's hot breathe on me, and realized, strange men and women, surrounded us with glowing orange eyes that shone through the darkness.

Chapter Two

James reached down and slid his hands over one another; He used his ring to cut open his palm, he forged a bloody dagger.

I reached up and touched the foreign woman's forehead and sent enough spider venom, which caused her to pass out and put her into temporary paralysis. Her hands seized, and fingers froze until she fell to the floor.

"Everyone wakes up; we're being invaded," I said. Ray, Toni, and Annabelle jutted awake.

Annabelle dragged her sword across the nearest man's arm, rich dark blood dripped to the ground and covered the blade.

Another orange-eyed man flung his wrist, which sent shards or slivers sailing through the air; one lodged itself deep into my forehead.

"Catalyst!" Ray screamed as he slid his hand and used his powers to turn the sliver kinetic energy to potential energy, and they fell to the floor.

James launched at the third man with his dagger and dug the blade deep into his skin, then the blood hardened further and shattered. The villain pulled chemical energy from James's body and blasted it back into him as thermal energy. James's arm burned, bubbled, and bled as he was thrown through the air and slammed against the wall.

Toni jumped up on to the third man's back and drew his handcrafted sword across his throat, barely drawing blood.

"ENOUGH EVERYONE DROP OR I WILL KILL YOUR FRIEND; I WANT ANSWERS WHO OR WHAT ARE YOU."

The lady woke up and put her hands up; she started to shoot sand from her hands. I grabbed her throat.

"If you like living, I would stop the sand show."

She fell to her knees, and we brought the other two over, tying all three of them together with rope from the ship.

"What are your names, what is your story? Why did you attack us?" I asked the one I presumed to be the leader.

"We come from Earth like you. We were banished long ago. They feared us and cast us out from the earth. The President of the United States said we were a threat to national security. I am Sandstorm, the tall Hispanic one with black hair and glasses is Sir Sliver. Sliver can touch certain items and weaken the bonds which leave shards or slivers that he can then shoot from his hands.

"The short, pudgy one with blonde hair is Thermal he can pull chemical energy from people and convert it and blast them with thermal energy. This planet has changed us tremendously besides these orange eyes that allow us to see in the dark, there are more of us back at camp that lost their powers altogether, some have been weakened and deteriorated by the planet enough to die or wish they could," said the strange woman. At that point I had already begun to feel her treachery. No one goes from trying to kill you to befriending you in five minutes. She was trying to hide something or desperately needed something.

Annabelle looked skeptical of the new orange-eyed woman.

"How long have you been here and how many of you are there, plus if you want us to trust you, maybe you should tell us your real name?"

The lady looked at her with a straight dead stare. "My name is Agatha; we don't know how long we've been here, time passes weird here we were exiled in 2105 what year is it now?"

James, Toni, and I looked at each other before responding. I looked at her, knowing she would be surprised,

"We left January 12th, 2125, which means you guys have been here for twenty years."

Before she could respond Toni motioned for me to come over, he cupped a hand around his lips and whispered into my ear "I know we got off on the wrong foot, I don't trust these people, and you should not either. They will double-cross you if they get what they want to remember. There is no loyalty among thieves. If it comes down to it, I will kill them; if it comes down to them or us, I'll save any of us first."

I looked over at Annabelle, who was sitting in the corner on a rock, focused on writing feverishly into a notebook.

"What are you working on? So intently?"

She looked almost annoyed. I'd asked, "I figured it would be a good idea to document our journey, plus it's like my journal, a journey journal."

I started to respond when Sliver jumped up suddenly, "Wait what's happened in the years we have been gone, I noticed on your suits it says NAC what is that?

I sat down next to Annabelle, and she rested her head on my shoulders. James, Toni, and Ray all sat down on the far side of the cave, and Agatha, Silver, and Thermal all sat down opposite of them; Thermal held Agatha's hand and used her chemical energy to create a weak thermal field which heated the cave and provided warmth.

"The United Nations held a summit to solve the world's problems they established a Union City to solve all the world's major problems, poor economies, homeless, crime.

It started with Europe; they combined communism and capitalism, democracy, and socialism. They created a centralized European government. Which spread the wealth, they employed the jobless and homeless to build homes they used the newfound wealth and knowledge to irrigate the deserts with seawater, fixed healthcare, criminals were sent to prison at sea until they could be rehabilitated. Threats were either killed or exiled to the Outland. It was so successful that each continent created a coalition that led to success. They claimed we have the lowest crime, no homeless, no poverty, and cheapest energy by using solar power, cleanest cities, and environments."

"Don't forget to mention how much bullshit that is, they lead the ignorant and kill or banish anyone who opposes them. Spend millions on propaganda. Nothing they said is true."

Annabelle stood up and whispered, "Hold on catalyst listen, do you hear that?" Ssssssssssssssssssss. I heard a high-pitched sound as if melting in a hot skillet.

"All hell!! We have to get out of here, or that stuff will eat your face all; we're going to have to get back to camp," shouted Sliver.

I saw Tiny pieces of pebbles fall from the ceiling; black ink colored liquid pushed through the walls and melted anything it touched. When it hit the floor, it splashed up, and a few drops hit the side of my face below my eye, I felt the liquid melt through my flesh and muscle down to the bone before it stopped. I started to scream, "AHHHHH LETS GET THE HELL OUTTA HERE. "

James, Toni, and Ray scrambled to get out of the door. Agatha, Sliver, and Thermal were almost out the door when turned toward the back wall that was melting, Agatha thrust her wrist shooting sand at the ooze and completely covered it. Thermal grabbed her hand, and she stopped producing sand. He started to blast the sand with heat hot enough to turn it to glass. Annabelle stood up and started to run out the door. Her foot caught a divot, and she fell to the ground, she screamed.

"What is that stuff, it's similar to lava it is black oozing acid?" Asked Toni.

Silver looked at him, running his hands through his beard.

"That is exactly it, it comes from deep under the planet's crust, in the outskirts of our camp it burst forth from the ground in geysers and will disintegrate anything it touches. We do not know what causes it; we have made use of it though, it heats our homes, and our camp is near the geysers because it keeps the beast and monsters out…"

Toni and I exchanged glances with James and Annabelle. None of us was sure what to make of these statements.

"Beast and monsters? What do you mean, what kind of beast and monsters?"

Thermal looked at me; the planet is filled with them, that's why we haven't been able to leave in all this time we have not been able to explore that much farther than our camp. We live of plants and lava lizards from the foot of the volcano, past the outer lands of our camp is where many monsters live, they are more like demons. Killing anything they touch; they say one of them has the power to rip the soul from your body. We have tried many times to pass the valley e time we lose a great many lives; there are not many of us left."

I looked over at Toni and James before I spoke as if we were reading each other's minds.

"Yes, before you did not have us brothers in blood and soon to be battle, we have powers, and yes, the battles will be difficult the harder the struggle, the greater it feels when you persevere, the longer and tougher the battle the greater our victory will feel. I say we go to your camp get your people and go to this wasteland fight the demons and then combine the working parts of both our ships and then figure out how to create fuel and go home and kill the tyrannous President. Who is with me? " I screamed with a rallying cry.

"Enough with the speeches man," said Toni

"You hate them now; I bet you will come around."

We packed what was left of our things, The cave and most of our stuff had been destroyed we still had several of Toni and Ray's handcrafted blades, a canteen that James had filled with the purple water, and bandages that Annabelle and I had crafted out of the cloth from the seats. The eight of us set out toward the camp. Agatha in the lead and Toni and Ray took up the flank. Toni had insisted on being in the rear because he had been in the military plus part of his powers knows military tactic of all time, so I choose not to argue.

We must have walked for miles and miles; I felt the bottoms of my spacesuit boots getting worn out.

"Guys, we're almost there. We're going to go up ahead and signal them." Said Agatha.

We watched as Agatha shot sand straight up into the air, in a single column a foot across. Thermal blasted it with his hands, which turned it to a glass cylinder, and Silver blasted it with slivers, which made it shatter and sent millions a piece of shattered glass everywhere.

An unfamiliar voice said,

"Sandstorm, Thermal, and sliver approaching!"

Agatha stepped forward and spoke.

"We have found new people. They have been banished – like us; they are going to help us get passed the demons and get home."

We stepped forward, and I saw an incredible wall; it stood at least 11 feet tall. It was made entirely of foreign bones and trees. One at a time, we stepped into a bone archway. It was made from a giant alien animal rib cage. After we stepped inside, I saw how bad off everyone was. People lied on the ground too weak to move. The planet had weakened them, mentally and physically, most of them malnourished. Annabelle and I climbed a spiraling tower, and we were able to see miles away. Every direction we looked all we saw were human Skeletons.

Annabelle sat down to write in her book, James and Ray walked upstairs to say goodnight and Agatha showed them which part of the fort they could sleep in.

"So, are you going to be ready for tomorrow? It's going to be dangerous, and it's different for us. We have powers. All you are going to have a sword, Annabelle." I said.

She set down her pen and book, and she walked over to me and looked into my eyes.

“I will be alright I can take care of myself plus I have you guys, I mean often I will probably be saving you guys. You know what I mean, though.” Annabelle said.

I glanced down at her beautiful face. My eyes lit up when I stared at her, and I said.

“Goodnight Annabelle gets some rest you will need it for tomorrow.”

I lay down on a bunch of wadded up shirts and gazed up at the foreign sky. I started to fall asleep when I heard a burning sound, and I saw smoke fills the air, I felt my eardrums ring when a man began to scream in the distance his voice shaking and filled with fear

“HE'S GOT ME. PLEASE HELP ME HE’S KILLING ME.”

I could only hear silence and then a thunderous roar echoing into the silence of the night.

Chapter Three

I awoke when I felt the warm sun heat up my face. I saw the bright morning lights peering over the walls of the fort. I lay on my back for a minute longer then went to check on Annabelle and the others. I heard the slow rhythmic breathing of Annabelle. For a moment, I looked upon her because, for a minute, she was peaceful and safe. Which I didn't think would happen for a long time

I heard Footsteps upon the stairs. The bone steps creaked one after another. I looked up, and I saw James standing in the doorway; his large build filling almost the entire frame, He walked over and sat next to me. At first, he looked over the fort before he spoke. He turned and looked into my eyes. When he spoke, his voice was shaky and filled with concern as deep as always. "Catalyst I remember years ago when I was working on a job site, my friend Charlie fell off the scaffolding and together with my friend George we caught him. We saved his life, and I never felt like a better person. We are supposedly Villains; sometimes, we do good things."

I interrupted him and shrugged my shoulders and ran my hand over my mouth and chin like I always do when I'm focusing.

"James, I struggle with being good or evil too. The thing is, I don't think there are good people, I think bad people do good things, and good people do bad things."

James looked at me with a questioned look on his face; he paused before answering.

"Well, I guess we'll see where life takes, whether we make good or bad decisions. I want you to know that no matter what happens I got your back; this journey is going to be rough, and I know we will not be able to save everyone. If it gets bad, I want you to save the others before me."

I started to interrupt him and tell him how ridiculous he was being; he raised his massive mitts to my mouth to quiet me. His face got serious, and his eye Narrowed.

"No, I am serious, when you get home, you need to tell my daughters that their daddy is a hero."

"James "

"Promise me!"

"Ok James, I promise they will know that their dad was a hero's hero and saved many lives. I promise I will do everything I can to get you home so you can tell them yourself."

James stood up and ran his ring over his palm and drew blood, he took my palm and slightly pressed his ring into my palm and scratched it across the top to bottom and then left to right forming a plus sign. He held his fist above my hand and then dropped a few drops of blood onto my palm. He reached his hand out and shook mine. He had clotted the blood on my hands.

"Through bloodshed, we are blood, "James chanted as he got up.

Toni's head popped in the doorway; he spoke with quickness and urgency.

"Agatha wants to leave in an hour she's getting her people ready now she suggests you do the same.

"Annabelle wakes up," I shook her awake.

"We have to get going, get your stuff, and round up all the people you can find, and if we have to fashion a few stretchers to carry the weak, we will have to do that too."

I headed down the stairs, James and Ray loaded people on to the stretchers, and Toni was sharpening the remaining swords. Sliver and Thermal walked over to Toni

"We have a gift for you; it's a sword made from the bones of the first-ever animal we killed."

The sword was about three feet long and was made from one solid bone, curved toward the front and doubled-edged.

Toni jumped up in wonderment and awe. "Oh my gosh, THANK YOU! It is like a cross between a Falcata of the ancient Celtiberians, the Romans Famed Gladius."

Toni practiced swinging its weight, and as he swung it underhand and overhand, it made a swooshing sound. He swung it with all his might and cut a tree trunk in half.

A loud echoing TWUNK rang out.

"Catalyst this time I will lead the way, you and Annabelle can lead from the rear, James you and Ray protect the left, and right flank, Agatha, Thermal, and sliver protect your people in the center. Let's move out people!"

Ray walked over to James and I and whispered.

"Guys who put this guy in charge. They gave him a fancy sword, and now he thinks he's Colonel badass."

I looked at James and the symbol on my palm

"Guys, don't worry, I'm in charge. I'm letting him lead because of his powers and military experience if I think he makes a bad call I'll call him out on it and take the lead again."

They looked satisfied enough for now as we existed the bone fort Agatha stopped for a second and looked back as if memories replayed in her head. She looked almost sad, she turned around and continuing to walk with the group.

We marched toward the unknown territories; we walked in perfect unison in unison as if all our arguing and fighting was over, and we were one. *Ba dum ba dum ba dum.* We began marching onward making small talk about passing the time. We entered a wooded area with strange black trees with dark grey leaves as tall as buildings the eerie razor wind licked and cutting our faces.

I smelt death and rotting flesh in the air.

We walked for several miles in silence; the only sound was the stomping pattern of our footfall on the ash-covered ground. The clouds of black soot being stirred up by the dozens of steps being taken. Annabelle caught up to me and opened her mouth to speak before she could start talking, Agatha shouted from up ahead.

"Catalyst we are nearing the edge of the woods on the other side are the outlands where there are tall grasses and fermenters. No one has ever survived a journey through the grasses. These demons feast on rotting flesh and can ferment your flesh."

Ray and sliver looked concerned and scared.

With an unsure voice, Ray stood in front of me and squared up his shoulders.

"We should go back! At least we won't be dead; even if we somehow make it home, they will lock us up or kill us. Here we will have a life even if the planet kills us. At least we will have a choice. Who's with me?"

Sliver was the only other person to step forward.

"Catalyst, Toni, he's right. We have lived on this planet for twenty years. Sure, it has been rough, and we have lost people we cared about at least we stayed alive. Agatha lets go back."

She pulled her hands away and shook her head.

"Live for how long, Sliver, a few miserable years — scrounging in the dirt like rats just waiting to die. That's not living. I'm going with them for a chance at life, and if you want to be a part of mine, I suggest you come with me."

They grew quiet and drifted toward the back of the group.

Everyone was edge and weapons were drawn, Toni unsheathed his bone sword and used his fingers to turn the sword in his wrist and swing it underhand.

He got in Ray's face and screamed loud and unwavering.

"Look, man I promised I would help catalyst get us home; we need you; when we get back to earth you can help us rule! Now I'm not asking you again come with us, or I will kill you"

Toni raised the sword above his head and started to bring it down on Ray. Ray jumped back and pushed his hand through the air turning Toni's energy from kinetic to potential, and Toni fell flat on his back. Agatha turned and blasted him with sand so powerful it pushed him six feet. His feet left miniature trenches in the dirt. James drew his mace, and I drew my sword.

I started to shout.

"Ugh, guys that's it I said no more fighting! I don't care if I have to start paralyzing people; we will not destroy our selves. We cannot make him come with us that it not right gives him a pack and let him go."

Ray hugged James and Annabelle goodbye, he went to shake hands with Toni pulled his hand away at the last second and stuck his middle finger in Toni's face. Sliver and Thermal handed him a pack and some rations; he turned and walked back toward Agatha's camp.

We marched on a little farther and stopped only to check on the weak. We were out of the woods, and I saw tall pointed grass and a low marsh. We pulled our swords out with a *Schuck* sound made by the swords being pulled from the handmade sheaths. I stepped into the swampy marsh. My footsteps displaced the water as I shuffled through the water. Close behind the man in front of me.

I smelt rancid rotting flesh. The stench started to overcome everything and filled my nostrils and burned my eyes.

I heard a deep roar and howling shrieking from a distance. The sloshing of water as if people running fast drew near.

"Guys, get ready. I raised my blade in anticipation. Everyone else did the same. Thermal and sliver raised their hands and fist ready to fight.

Annabelle stood in front of James and I. Her fingers curled around her book as well as her sword, and her knuckles turned white. Beast emerged from the tall grasses and began to surround us. They resembled giant dogs the size of bears their fur ink black and their eyes and dark orange.

I yelled, "This is it. We can get past this beast and triumph. We must all attack at once!

A fermenter leaped toward Agatha and the others near her she blasted him back with sand, Thermal began shooting energy to heat her sand. A second beast ran toward James and I; I lunged at him bringing my sword down on his neck. The monster looked up and absorbed it into his body! It rusted metal and spit the pile of dust and ash to the floor. James forged a blood dagger into the fermenter's skull, blood oozed and poured forth from his mouth. The monster bucked and sank his teeth deep into James's massive forearm. It depleted his arm's blood of oxygen and sugar in his blood turned to carbon dioxide, which fermented his arm and rotted his flesh and turned his skin into a deep purple and black and had almost reached his shoulder. James screams took over everyone's ears.

Toni ran over and screamed

"There is only one thing to do now as the military would say.

"Save life over limb."

He swung the bone sword and cut James' arm clean off. James screamed in agony.

"AAAAHHHHHHHHHHH WHAT THE HELL."

Then he passed out from shock.

The fermenters started coming again and again. Another fermenter leaped on top of me, and I smelt death on his breath. The beast dug his claws deep into my legs and another set into my chest, then it began to ferment my body. He bent down to close his jaws on my throat. He got closer and closer. I placed my hand on his chest and filled his chest with box jellyfish poison, instantly killing it. His corpse fell to the floor. I grabbed James's knife and used it to cut the rot out of my leg and chest.

I fell to the ground, weak and exhausted. Another fermenter had started to attack Agatha and sliver. The animal clawed at Agatha; she blasted him with sand, he shook it off as if it were dust. I stood up to help fell to my knees once again. Sliver had reached down to touch one of the dead fermenters and shot slivers of their bones back at the fermenter that attacked Agatha. The bone slivers pierced the fermenter's eyes. The monster seemed Unfazed he barreled along after them when a second creature came. They pounced on Sliver and bit and clawed at him. His body's oxygen escaped. Then his body fermented like alcohol; the sugar turned into carbon dioxide, his organs pickled and burst open as his entire body turned purple and black and he fell to the ground his screams were animalistic as he died. More fermenters came, and with James and me weak, our rear and right flank was exposed and vulnerable.

Herds of the demons had broken our lines, and I had begun to lose consciousness when I saw the fermenters ravage the men and women of Agatha's exiled crew.

Dozens of them died horrifying deaths. One fermenter leaped upon Annabelle; She grabbed James's discarded mace and dipped it into the dead fermenter's chest of poison. With one mighty swing, she sang it into the fermenter's skull.

I looked around at the dozens of fermenter dogs that surrounded us, and we're about to kill my friends. I knew what I had to do, well if I could do it. I had only blown disease spores once. I used every ounce of strength in my body on a maybe. I filled the air with an incredible amount of canine distemper enough to kill 500 regular dogs. It killed a good many of them. Toni and Annabelle sliced through the rest. The *thwack* of their blades easily cut through the weakened fermenters. I helped Annabelle to her feet, and Thermal started to help Agatha up when a fermenter bigger than all the rest rose from the ashes. I felt the heat emitting from the ashes and the fermenting purple bloated bodies. A strange gravelly animalistic voice started to speak.

"You may have killed the animals, my underdogs. It will not be so easy to kill me. I am a true demon above demons; these beast bodies serve me well for feasting and a host body. I possess one of them until they die and then I possess another. They serve me phenomenally."

There were a few of us left — Agatha, Thermal, James, Toni, Annabelle, and a few of the powerless exiled ones. We circled Annabelle and the people who had lost their powers. Toni raised his bone blade to the sky in anticipation.

"Annabelle! Catch!" I yelled.

I threw her a sword from one of the fallen men. She stood back to back with me, ready to battle. The Demon stood to his feet and was ready to kill. Blood dripped from his teeth and onto the floor.

I shouted with intensity and unwavering need.

"Everyone attack now, it has to be all at once!"

The beast gained speed as he ran for us. Thermal blasted him with thermal energy. Agatha began to blast him with sand. He shook it off as if none of it fazed him.

The attacks went through his ghostly figure one at a time. The fermenter demon pushed his hand through one of the exiled men's bodies. His paws pushed through the man's chest. It killed him and turned his body into a pile of purpled bloody flesh and rot. Toni raised his blade to strike the demon and slashed the blade through the air.

The demon phased through the ground. He emerged from the ground below Agatha's feet and grabbed her legs then sank his claws into her ankles.

"No, I see now that there is only one way."

Thermal threw himself into the demon's fermenter form and tried to push the demon out. Toni slit the fermenter's throat and cut off his head. The demon was free and formless. It latched onto Thermal. They wrestled for control of the body.

"If you need a host body, then take mine." Thermal dived into the marshy water and drowned himself while heating the water to boil his body.

The rest of us stood there with our mouths agape, barely able to comprehend everything that had happened. We stood there for several minutes, trying to make sense of all the events. Agatha cried and mourned for her best friends, who were lost. She walked over to me and slapped my hand across the mouth. It was hard enough to echo in the distance.

She was angry and sad and shouting through her tears.

"This is all your fault!

"They are dead because of you! You promised we would all get to go home!"

"Ray was right. Some leaders you are, we barely got anywhere, and two-thirds of us are dead!" Her face was red hot, and her spit was flying.

She pressed her face into Slivers' dead body and cried into his bloody chest.

"Of course, you wanted to go through none of your people died! I have almost no people left. You used their dead bodies as a steppingstone to carry you and your friends to safety."

She frantically dug up dirt with slivers sword so she could bury the dead. Dirt and dark grass were frantically thrown into the air.

I kneeled beside her and wrapped my arms around her.

"I am sorry for the loss of your friends truly. I am! If we could have made it through without their deaths, I would have taken that route; they had to die so that we could live. They knew the dangers, and I'm the one who saved you and everyone I killed nearly all the fermenter dogs. Thermal killed the demons, and for this, I am grateful. Let's get one thing straight change is inevitable I won't be the same person when this is over, and neither will you. Now let's move out. We will grieve later."

James helped her to her feet, and they started to move out. Toni gathered the swords and put them in his pack. He spun his sword through the air and took the point once again. He sharpened his sword and wiped the blood off as he went. Annabelle walked next to me and spoke slowly and thoughtfully.

Annabelle walked by me, and my eyes lit up. Damn, she was beautiful. Despite all the tragic events, I still managed to crack a smile.

She turned at the last second and flipped her hair.

"I guess that trick with the airborne dog disease was pretty cool; I mean not as cool as when that one with a mace, it was still pretty cool."

"Hey James, you're going to be alright I know it's one thing to die in battle. It's another altogether to live be missing an arm," I said.

He looked at his shoulder longingly as if wanting it back enough would bring it back. He spoke hesitantly and sad.

"It's as if I can still feel pain in it. My arm is fucking gone, and I wish I could feel the pain in it. I will be fine at least I'm alive I'll still give them a hell of a fight."

Toni and I picked up the stretcher and carried the wounded. We marched forward toward were no one had ventured before.

Chapter Four

Night had fallen. We wanted to put more distance between us and where we had slain the fermenters and the Demon king. We traveled in painful silence. We mourned the lost and the wounded. We were one step closer toward getting back to earth and being free. What would it cost us? Everything? Everyone?

I heard a familiar sizzling sound, so I looked at the ground. The acid-like lava slivered downhill and into a black lagoon. It churned and boiled and rumbled. The steam burned upon my arm. An acid geyser shot a hundred feet into the air. We bent down to shield our necks. James and I wrapped our bodies around Agatha, Annabelle, and Toni.

The other exiled ones from Agatha's crew had not caught up to us yet. James and I felt It splash my skin. It took it's time as it burnt trails into my skin as it rolled down my back. My eyes tightened, and my veins popped out of my head as I screamed out in pain.

"AHHHH HOLY CRAP AAAAAAAAA"

I fell to my knees as the geyser began to retract back into the ground. I looked around and saw bits of metal and other debris.

I winced in pain and spoke in short sharp breaths.

"Hey Toni, can you check out that, Debris field."

Toni walked over to the biggest chunk of metal and flipped it over. We all stared in awe and disbelief, the piece of metal had part of an ancient logo of the Earth's space program and the words: THE ECLIPSE.

Toni looked puzzled and started to stare at Agatha questioningly.

"Hey Agatha," Toni paused as he asked, trying to word his question particularly.

"So, if you're telling the truth about your ship and where you landed and all of this, then what is this wreckage from? This logo Is too old to have been the one that brought you?"

Agatha was pissed, especially at being falsely accused. She got in Toni's face and shot sand into his face.

She screamed Angrily and shaky, her eyes scrunched, and her shoulders raised back.

"Look Toni boy because there are bits of a ship is scattered here does not mean I lied or that I am withholding information. DO NOT ACCUSE ME OF LYING AGAIN!

Hello, we passed my ship by the fort. We were foolish to think because no more ships ever came near us that no more were sent here.

Obviously, depending on what time of year and day the ships launched would change where they landed."

Toni and I exchanged glances as if to agree with how we had been stupid. He looked almost apologetic as he walked over to Agatha.

"I am truly sorry that I accused you of lying and everything else, one question that still needs to be answered if you didn't come on this ship someone else did, and I think we should find out who."

James, who had been silent for a while and tended to the other people, ran over to us with a shocked look on his face.

He opened his mouth and through quick panting breaths, forced out a sentence.

"Hey guys you are never going to believe this, Me and Annabelle saw something swimming in the acid."

I turned to ask him about it when I felt a sudden breeze passed over me and heard a loud whoosh *THUD* behind me. A dead growly voice began to speak. A hand clamped down on my shoulder. The fingers all came to points like the talons of a hawk.

"Hello, and who might you be, more newcomers from Earth perhaps."

I looked around; we had been surrounded. Each of these strange men had the bodies of humans, except they had heads like dragons with dark solid black eyes with bright red centers — sunken in ears and bright hollow crest on top of their heads. Scales covered them from head to toe. The one thing the lacked was a nose. Where it should have been was merely a hole. He had begun to speak his mouth again gigantic, and his teeth pointed like daggers and just about as big.

"Do not be afraid of us; if you do not incite violence, neither shall we."

The men that had surrounded us launched themselves into the air with large and powerful wings that had extended from their backs. Then slammed onto the ground next to us. They watched us curiously.

"We arrived on the planet three-night falls ago, Agatha and the others in her group crashed here about twenty years before us. Now that we told you our story, let's hear yours."

The strange man stroked his claws across his dragon-like face.

"A long time ago back before the years of great change that reshaped the government, the United States and the European Union, along with the rest of the world. They had a secret program called project sunshine, where they used dead bodies to test radiation on. However, when they tested it on us, we were only in a deep comatose state and not dead.

When we awoke, we all had radiation racked bodies; we were burned, charred, and disfigured. Our blood and fluids leaked everywhere. So, the governments did what they knew they had to do to cover up everything. They shipped us off along with several other "science projects and lab mishaps." Anyway, our ship crashed into this acid lake It fused the liquid to our radiation-soaked bodies along with the oil and various other things. It turned us into theses freaks you see today. We are basically dragons, we can fly, and we look like dragons instead of fire. We can spew black acid from our mouths. It's truly remarkable; it is capable of melting almost anything."

I looked up at the man in awe and disbelief. I spoke thoughtfully.

"I am truly sorry about all that messed up stuff that happened to you, you still never told us your names or what you want from us. "

The dragon-man began to speak again.

"My name is Gabriel; the others are Smith and Willard. We only want revenge against the people that sent us here, and if not them, then their children or their children's children shall pay." He snarled.

James spoke up and interrupted Gabriel.

"Sir, we are not Villains. We want to save the world from the tyrannical rule of our time. What you propose would punish innocents for their ancestor's crimes. While we understand that what they did to you is horrific, we cannot condone what you propose."

Smith spoke up his voice low and dragged as if every word were trying to catch on to everything.

"Look, big man; we were not asking for permission. We were telling you what we are going to do."

The third man, Willard, put his hand out to Toni, Toni shrugged his shoulders and pushed his hands away.

"While our end goals do not match exactly. We all want relatively the same things, to leave this planet to go home and to seek revenge.

If we work together, we can forge a ship from the wreckages of our vessels and however many more groups have crashed here," said Smith

Agatha, Toni, and I huddled together with James and Annabelle. I spoke with a hurried and hushed tone.

"Can we really consider helping to bring these monsters to earth, who knows what they can do. What powers they are not telling us about."

Toni stared off into space. His face frozen and focused, and I assumed that's what it looked like when he was examining and exploring e event and the battle of history. He broke from his trance and began to speak.

"Catalyst in World War II, the former United States, Had a nonaggression pact with the Russians they weren't necessarily allies because they did not trust them or share common goals, they agreed not to fight each other and to fight the Germans instead," Toni said.

I thought for a moment before responding and running my hand over my mouth and chin.

I asked Toni, "So you're saying we shouldn't trust them, the whole the enemy of the Enemy of my friend thing."

Annabelle spoke up sharply.

"Guys I agree with you; however, if we are going to keep finding more groups of people, I think we should be in charge and vote on the things we do."

I glanced around at all the faces that surrounded me. They all seemed to agree except Agatha, who was agitated. She hissed and shouted in a whisper; her shoulders rose as she squared up the group.

"No, trusting them is a bad idea, it will cost us lots. We should not have to vote on this if we do not kill them now, they will surely kill us when we give them what they want. Which will mean all of my friends and people died in vain."

I heard the mighty flapping of wings, and then Gabriel landed near us. He approached us, angry and agitated.

"Enough talking, we are coming with your end of the story, either you go along with it, or we kill you all. He grabbed hold of Toni's arm, and he presses his finger against Toni's dark skin. I tried to counter with poison as fast as I could. Smith grabbed my wrist. Willard grabbed James and Annabelle. With her sandblast Agatha propelled herself into the air and beyond the reach of the dragon men.

She began to scream.

"I told you not to trust them! Now beast let go of my friends, or you will perish. "

The dragons laughed at Agatha, shrugged off her threat. Agatha twisted her fingers and flicked her wrist. The ground under Smith gave way and turn into quicksand. He sank into the ground.

Gabriel spit onto the floor, it let go of Toni.

"Agatha, it is too late, child. I have poisoned you all especially the poisoner."

"You see part of Project sunshine was the scientists were testing the effects of Strontium 90. Part of our powers is that we can excrete it into the bodies of others. The chemical seeks out bones and bone marrow, and it can cause bone cancer however we can control it in your body and simply kill you at will now back down girly."

I fell to my knees in pain. My bone marrow poisoned, and I fell unconscious from the pain. I awoke, being dragged along. James was in front of Annabelle and me behind. I looked at Toni to my side. Annabelle asked

"Gabriel, you said you poisoned us. That since you can kill us if we don't do what you say you'll kill us? "

I glanced over at Toni, Annabelle, and James. I nodded and crossed my arms, and sent the opossums natural anti-venom into my bloodstream. I noticed if I stretched, I could barely reach Annabelle's hand. I extended my arm and scratched her, then sent the anti-venom into her bloodstream. I screamed as I saw James fall to his knees because he was having a hard time with his powers since he lost his arm and so much blood. The poison was getting to him. I stood up.

I was so mad I felt my jaw pop from clenching my teeth so tight. I went to reach for Smiths' leg; Gabriel shot up and spit the black acid all over my hand. I saw it meet my flesh. It was so hot that my skin boiled before melting off and splattering to the floor. The tissue and muscle were burned through next. The pain was almost unbearable. It was so painful I could not scream my body frozen from shock.

Gabriel leaned back to blast me again when he was knocked back. He then grew limp and plummeted to the floor.

"You guys look like you could use some positive energy and help," said a familiar voice.

I looked up and saw Raymond. He walked closer toward us. I stood up and shook his hand before turning to help James to his feet. I heard the familiar sound of a blade being drawn from a sheath. Annabelle and Agatha have drawn their swords. James grabbed Gabriel by his ankle and threw him at my feet. Smith had tried to fly behind us. Agatha blasted Toni into the air, and he caught Smith by surprise then sent his bone sword deep into the man's back.

I grabbed Gabriel's leg and sent King cobra venom into his blood.

I looked at him, then at Smith and Willard.

"That's it, no more fighting. If we work together, we could be an unstoppable group. Mr. Gabriel, if you submit to a truce, so will we, and I will give you the anti-venom for that cobra poison."

He looked reluctant; his jaw was locked, he said.

"We will enter a temporary truce; the minute we land on earth all bets are off. "

The team and I all nodded in agreement. Raymond approached me and whispered in my ear. He said

"Catalyst, the reason I came after you is because I went back to Agatha's fort, and I saw a drawing of that dragon dude. If they had not been past the fermenters how did she know about them."

I looked up at Agatha, talking to Annabelle. They both smirked and went back to talking. I turned back to Ray again, and I said.

"Thank you for letting me know I think we should wait to worry about her until Gabriel and his goons are under control."

We walked into the darkness, and we walked in silence once more. Toni and I helped James walk. He had grown weak due to the extreme loss of blood from his missing arm. Gabriel and I walked over to James, and I could see him grab James' stumped shoulder into his hands.

"Either get him fixed or cut him off. We need to hurry up, or by the time we get back, even more time will have passed may be too late to stop this total global government.

"I shoved him and said, "Listen dude. If you don't step off James, I will break our deal and make sure you are within an inch of your life for days before you die. Now let's keep moving maybe there is another crash site that we can get parts from maybe, even something to help James"

Gabriel scoffed and flew to the front, taking point next to Toni. Agatha and Smith were behind him, and Willard and Annabelle behind them. James and I covered the rear flank. The group walked further into the darkness and the planet.

Chapter five

Crunch crunch. The dark black and grey leaves cracked and crushed underfoot. We had walked for almost an entire day. My legs grew tired and weak. I looked around at everyone else, shuffling along and breathing heavily. No one wanted to stop and make camp for fear of being killed by each other or at least a long, drawn-out fight. The hope was still alive. I hope that we could find another ship and fix our own. Hope we could find shelter and food and clean water.

"Guy's, we are going to have to rest if we don't stop soon; we're not going to make it that much farther," I said.

We approached an ink-black lagoon shaded by big jagged dark trees. The canopy made the area cooler by about ten degrees. James sunk to his knees and almost passed out. With short narrow breaths, he said l.

"If I don't rest here, I'll probably pass out in a few more steps, this clearing is nice, let's take a breather."

Gabriel sighed loudly and rolled his eyes while walking over to us. He said.

"We can stop here for a little while if we don't attack you, you can't attack us now we are going to go look for some food. Smith, Willard, and I also Agatha should come too. We have a history of mutilating our prey."

Agatha glanced over at me, and her eyes conveyed worry with strategy. She said

"Sure, I'll come with you guys, back on Earth I use to go hunting with my friends all the time as a kid."

They had packed some bags with the rope, a knife, and more gear. They started to head off toward the west, where Gabriel said he had heard some grunting.

Before they disappeared over the cliff through the black trees, I shouted.

"Agatha, be careful, come back to us in one piece!"

She smiled, nodded, and walked off into the distance. I sat down next to James and Toni.

Annabelle and Toni had started to walk and talk. Their conversation grew distant as they walked to the other side of the lagoon. I took a seat next to James and Ray. I was nervous, and I chewed on my tongue I glanced across the lake at Annabelle. The sight of her made my eyes light up, and I felt a smile start to crack on my face.

"You like her, don't you dude? I can tell you go from this badass warrior to this cheesy lovesick guy."

I turned around, James had stood up and was leaning against the tree.

I sighed, "Well, I think it's stupid to say you like someone you met; we are not in high school, man. I think she is attractive. Yes, I think she's sweet and cool, I barely know her so how I can like her."

I could not believe the cheese I had spouted or how I was somehow this immature yet mature and badass guy.

"If you don't hurry up and step it up, Toni's going to step in and take your girl, "said Ray.

Squeak, squeak, squeak A Strange animal galloped through the woods and knocked me down to my knees. It was the size of a small deer, with dark red fur and a long trunk-like snout. It reminded me of one of those crazy aardvarks.

"GET HIM!"

Shouted Gabriel as he busted through the trees and flew faster and faster. I stood up and made a dive for the aardvark deer landed flat on my chest.

Agatha said, "He is too fast we couldn't catch him, we steered him toward you guys; someone gets him."

James Dragged his ring across his stomach and dripped a few drops into his fingers. He rolled his finger together and formed his blood into a dart. He tossed it to me, and I ran the dart through my fingers and covered it with a small amount of tarantula toxin. I threw it into the air to Annabelle. She caught it and threw it into the animal's neck, which killed it. Gabriel and his friends landed on the ground and tied up the animal and dragged him through the woods. The group walked again after waiting a while.

I heard a soft metallic echo as if I walked on a tin roof. The smell of grease and old engine parts wafted through the air and filled my nostrils. I dropped to my hands and knees and shifted the dirt out of the way. I saw dark white metal under the black earth.

"Guys help me dig; it's a ship; we could be saved! "I said.

Gabriel, Smith, and Willard joined talons and shot into the sky.

Gabriel said, "Stand back Catalyst, I will take care of it since you can't."

They continued to blast the dirt with their acid breath until it melted through the dirt like nothing before it could eat through the metal hull. They sucked it back into their bodies. The acid was so hot I felt the warmth radiate off the ship onto my face.

The acid had unearthed. The ship had also perfectly formed a crater at least twenty feet across.

"Catalyst, you want to go exploring?" Annabelle asked.

She looked at me, her eyes sparkled, and she was excited. I smiled back at her, and we started to walk toward the crater. Toni and Ray grabbed the net from Gabriel's pack and lowered Annabelle and I into the crater. Gabriel, Smith, and Willard flew Agatha down to the ship. I said, "Toni and Ray, you guys stay here and look out for threats."

When our feet touched the floor of the crater, we walked around the new ship when Annabelle shouted.

"Catalyst look at this, the names partially scrubbed off, it says the Orion. Dssssss Clunk Gabriel sunk his talons into the door and ripped it clean off the hinges.

I said, "dude, what are you doing if we could have used this ship before there is no way we can now rip the door off!!"

Gabriel stepped up to me and bowed up his chest as he extended his talons.

"Well "dude" last I checked you're not my boss you have a problem fight me then. Otherwise, shut up."

"Are you mocking me, dragon boy?"

I stood up next to him and pushed my chest against his, my hands ready to strike poison into his bloodstream. Annabelle wedged her way in between us.

"If you guys don't stop fighting, we will never get off this planet. Now let's go into the ship."

Toni started shouting from above, "Wait, did you guys say the Orion? As in the project from the fifties in the former United States. They used a string of nuclear bombs to propel the ship into space. However, the government said it was an unfeasible idea that was unpopular with public opinion due to nuclear fallout and scrapped it."

Toni opened his mouth to speak again. A loud sound started to emit from inside the ship. *Beep, beep, beep*, the noise went for ten seconds and then shut off. Gabriel stepped into ships doorway and said cockily

"Well, I don't know about you guys I'm going to go be the guy who finds the way and saves Everyone."

I ducked my head under the archway of the door and into the ship. I pushed past Gabriel and toward the Beeping sound. The others had joined us as we made our way through the winding hallways of the ship, venturing further and further. The ship grew dim the farther away we got from the broken door.

I heard the metal creak with each step; Toni draws his bone sword. A loud voice blared from the darkness, and a bright screen turned on from the wall.

"Hello, if you hear this congratulation on not dying because it means we have. The planet is filled with endless amounts of danger. Within the first five days, my Ten-man crew had been killed by everything from razor wind and acid lakes to strange creatures and beast. My wife and copilot Margret were the last to die before me. She was driven mad by the deaths of the crew and the betrayal by the governments who sent us here. Project Orion was a Top-secret mission, so no one knew that it had secretly been built. When the public scrutiny Grew too much due to the fear of radiation fallout, the public was told the project was merely an idea and had not begun to be built. However, the government knew it had to cover up the work as well as get their monies worth. They told us in the mission briefing that our goal was to prove to the world that the nuclear bomb powered spacecraft was the future and that the planet held a cure to radiation poisoning.

However, it turned out we were the second government cover-up sent to this planet to be out of the public eye because when we arrived, the mission we received was to survive. We were told the reason we were able to use nuclear-powered bombs to push the ship was that they had tested the radiation on living people before and blasted them into space a few years before, and they had survived. It turned out they had attempted to test dead bodies, and a few of them happened to be alive. They pretended that it was an accident that it was a mistake, it wasn't. They were testing to find people they could send to space and would live. We figured out when we got here that they had lived alright, they had been covered up and sent to die here like us. We attempted to repair our ship without fuel or replacements for the damaged parts we were stranded.

We are left to die. If you're watching this message, avenge us and kill the bastards responsible. In the next room, I left what few supplies we had a burner and few other things. As I write this the monsters close in on me."

The video depicted a strange giant dinosaur-like beast bashing through the door and feasting on his body as his bloody body parts were strewn about.

Agatha spoke up first, "Damn guys, that's crazy I think maybe we should turn it off now. Like, guys, that's disgusting, let's take the supplies, the parts and go."

Gabriel grabbed her wrist before she turned on the video.

"Whoa girl, why you in such a hurry to go."

The room on the video was filled again when Agatha and Thermal and Splinter filled in to search the room. We watched in silence as they emptied the room of everything and dragged away from the man's body. The scream dimmed and shut off completely. Smith and Ray spoke up first enemies that had a new equal feeling of hate and distrust. They pushed Agatha to the floor. Gabriel screamed, "You continue to lie, girl. You lied to them. You lied to us. You knew they existed which means you knew we existed, and you helped us not. Why should we not kill you right now!"

James and I looked at each other in agreement. I said, "let her go, Gabriel, Ray back down now!" I placed my hand on Gabriel's arm, and James drew a blood shaped sickle to Ray's throat.

"THAT'S ENOUGH I'm in charge. We will settle this civilly. This is not the old west; we all have questions we want to answer our selves. We will not survive by killing one another. Now Agatha explains yourself."

Agatha wiggled and writhed out of the men's grasp. She started in a slow whisper, then threw her hands about wildly and shouted. Agatha said

"We were dying; I had already watched dozens of my friends die horrid deaths. I knew I had to save them! Had to save us! One day A ship fell from the sky. Before it even crashed to the ground, we were waiting. We knew we had to kill them before they killed us. So, we made sure the beast and the dinosaurs, the acid, and the planet were dealt with. We would use their ship to escape and be saved. Then she had it broken, she killed the remaining people, and she sealed off this place with the fermenters. I am sorry that I didn't tell you all this before I promise I stand with you Catalyst I won't betray you and I'll do whatever you need me to get me home, don't let them kill me ."

I pondered everything she said and questioned everything she had told me before. While it answered some things, it opened more questions. Who's this mysterious lady, how can we beat her, and why does she want people to forever stay on this planet. I wanted to ask her all of this and more alas I was hungry, and we had that aardvark thing to eat. We'd have time to figure this stuff out later. So, I looked at Agatha in her eyes and said.

"The only reason I'm letting you stay with us and not leaving you here alone is that I made a promise that I would get you off this planet, and I will keep that promise you do what I say. "Gabriel, Smith, Willard, Ray, and Toni all drew their weapons.

"She is a traitor. She would have killed us! Better her than us." Gabriel said

I said, " No you are not going to kill her, she has fought side by side with us, she could have let us die many times; she has lost more than all of us if you want to kill her you'll have to go through us."

I drew my sword and got my hand ready. James raised his sickle again poised to slash. Annabelle raised her sword and stood in front of Agatha. The room grew quiet; you heard a slow drip of water echoing through the ship. I began to speak

"once again, here is what's going to happen..." Gabriel cut me off and slashed his talons in the air attempting to slice my face open. I grabbed his arm and twisted it, pushing Komodo dragon venom into his skin and with it the lizard's immobilizing agent. Smith and the rest of the men were taken aback. Toni crossed over and stepped beside me and said.

"That is why he's the boss, I guess." I touched Gabriel again and withdrew my poison from his vein and body. He slumped to the floor and passed out. I was breathing heavy, and I felt beads of sweat rolling down my forehead.

"Now Smith, you and Ray go drag in that Aardvark start up the stove and cook that damn thing. Toni, you and Willard, figure out a way to get James a new arm or something."

He paced the cabin for a while. He walked from one end of the room to another. Then he stopped, and his eyes lit up his brain replayed memories of battles and wars through his own eyes as if he were there.

"THAT'S IT!"

Toni said as he jumped excitedly. He ran through the ship's rooms. He rummaged through the mostly empty cabinets and hatches. He screamed with excitement when he pulled out a 3D printer, and he turned it on. It buzzed and shook free cobwebs and dust.

"Back in 2046 Japan grew frustrated when they realized it had been a hundred years since they had been beaten by the allies in WW2 they claimed they needed to Invade China for something, anyway long story short they militarized their police force and the Police chief lost his arm in battle so they 3D printed him a new one.".

James stepped over to where Toni was standing, he uncovered his shoulder stub, and after a great while, Toni was able to 3D print him a new arm. Annabelle was excited. She raced for the control panel of the ship and wedged her blade inside and pulled out wires and parts. Gabriel walked over reluctantly and said.

"If I offer a mere drop of acid small enough to melt the wires, you're using not destroy them, will that be helpful?"

Agatha was focused and flying. She and Gabriel Worked together, and after a while, they took the 3D printed arm and handed it back to James. They Attach the wires to his arm, and the other half lead up to a helmet. When James placed it on his head his brain sent impulses to the arm, and he could control the arm and hand. He was floored with excitement he jumped in the air and began to dance around thanking everyone for all they had done.

I smelt the aardvark like animal toasting in the next room, and then they brought it in and for the first time since we had gotten to this planet. We had a good time we gathered around a Conference table in one of the rooms of the ship. We ate, and we talked, and we had a good time.

We bonded, and we got to know each other more. Until Gabriel turned to Agatha and asked her the question, all of us had wanted to ask her we were avoiding.

"Who was this lady you spoke of before, this big bad. Killing and plotting and puppeteering if she even exists at all. You were probably lying about her like everything else."

Agatha stood up and slammed the table, shoving her food to the floor and got in his face.

"You are the liar! She is real, and you know if she calls herself the goddess of suffering, and she can kill you any way she likes by barely touching you, some say she plays with her victims testing out different ways of torture and death with each new person. She never uses the same method to kill twice."

I stood up and raised my glass of purplish water in the air.

"If she is real, we will kill her, the fermenters were impossible to beat, and we beat them the demon could not be downed we defeated him we can conquer her if we work together! Now let's get some rest so in the morning we will grab what we can carry or what we think we can use to fix the *Mach infinity*."

We all headed toward different areas of the Orion and laid down. Annabelle followed James and me, and we found spots in a room that appeared like it had been the kitchen. Of course, Gabriel and his friends took the bunks. Toni and Ray were first up to keep watch outside the ship. Annabelle walked over to me.

"Hey, Catalyst? Do you think you and I could cuddle; you know for the warmth of course

I smiled, and my eyes lit up, and I felt my cheeks get warm.

"Of course, we can cuddle I would love that, for warmth, of course."

Annabelle and I had laid down together, and as she laid on my chest, I wrapped my arms around her. We had begun to drift off to sleep when I remembered I hadn't thanked her for helping James.

"Hey, Annabelle? Thank you for helping James and especially for helping to create that bad-ass new arm. I had no idea you were that good with inventing stuff or technology."

"Hey Catalyst, I think it is weird that everything is happening so easily. Catching that random animal, not only finding this ship it is fully functional. Not to mention the fact that a video we need to see happens to be the first thing to play. I would have to say the craziest thing was when Toni, a random guy was able to create a new, fully functional arm with little trouble. I can't even make a wooden box without running into a problem."

"Annabelle, what are you saying? Someone has been able to not only influence what happens to us is using that to make our lives easier. I'm sorry I don't think that is possible."

She sighed and turned away from me. After a few minutes I began to think about all the thoughts running through my head. Could I trust Agatha? What about Gabriel, Willard, or Smith? Would I be able to kill them after fighting side by side with them? Am I a good guy now? I was a bad guy. I'm tired of hurting people I could have. I have great friends, and I feel like Annabelle, and I could go somewhere. I scratched my face, and I felt a cut slice across my chin, and I looked down, and I saw what I tried so hard to forget. I ran my good hand across my cold burnt hand and forearm – not even a thin layer of charred tendons covering the bone. I shed a single small tear and felt it roll softly down my cheek. After a little while longer. My mind finally settled, and I drifted off to sleep.

Chapter six

I jolted awake when Toni shouted.

"Hey, Catalyst, it's time for you and James to be on lookout duty!"

"Hey man, quiet down Annabelle's sleeping dude," I said.

I heard someone scribbling feverishly on paper. I looked up, and I saw Annabelle was mesmerized by her work.

"Annabelle? "I asked, what are you doing up it's the middle of the night?"

She set her pen down and leaned her head back.

"I couldn't sleep; writing is my favorite thing. My mom always said, "Writing is your superpower; when you write anything can happen. You can make everything end up the way you want it to."

She smiled and started to write again.

"Wow that's inspiring, your mom sounds like a smart lady."

James stood up and pulled me to my feet.

"It's time to go, dude, we have to keep watch," James said.

We walked toward the door when James put his arm in front of my chest.

"Shhh listen," he said.

The hair on my neck stood up, and a shiver ran down my spine. The unfamiliar voice of a lady spoke slow and like a demon.

"So, you are the new people trespassing on my planet. Like many before you, I will enjoy killing you one at a time. Savoring the sound of your screams and the sweet gasp of your last breath."

I stood with my mouth agape. For once in my life, I knew what fear was.

"Uh, James," I asked hesitantly, "what the hell was that."

I saw the fear on James' face. He was so scared he couldn't speak. I slapped him out of it. He came around and opened his mouth to speak; no words came out. A rustling came from behind James and me.

Agatha stepped out into the light. She spoke quietly so that the others wouldn't hear.

"I wanted to wait until the three of us could talk in private because I don't trust anyone else, yes I'll admit I was bad, and I let her kill people so that my people could live. When I met you guys, I knew I could not let you die. I was a disciple for the Duchess of death. This time we go to her. We fight, and we win! "Said, Agatha.

James stood up and his massive frame towering over Agatha and me.

James said, "Agatha when we go to fight this demon witch lady or whatever I'll be right by your side if we can't get off this planet we might as well stay here sucking down aardvark creatures with purple sludge water. I suggest we scrap the usable parts and Take them with us until we can find some fuel source to take us out of here."

Gabriel walked through the door, pissed, and slammed stuff around.

"Glad to know we're a Team Catalyst you guys are over here having secret meetings without me, I moved here trying to save us all. I was able to salvage the liquid fuel valve. You know how hard it is to pop one of those off with a sword and a claw."

I walked over to Gabriel and Agatha and folded my arms while I stroked my chin.

"Look, I'm sorry we didn't include you; I thought you were sleeping, you know since it's the middle of the night. Silly me. All that happens was we heard the voice of some crazy duchess of death who promised to kill us all and enjoy doing it and that James wants to scrap this ship ASAP. I promise we will include you from now on. Let's get started on grabbing parts."

I extended my hand out and shook Gabriel's clawed hand. He didn't look pleased with least it shut him up. The four of us started to walk outside when the rest of the group joined us. Our trust issues had grown high. Gabriel, Smith, and Willard flew to the top of the crater forming an assembly line style of disassembling the ship. Toni pried up a chunk of paneling with his bone sword. They are carefully severing bolts and screws while trying not to slice wires. Ray turned the fuel tanks' potential energy into kinetic energy, and it began to slide and move. James and Ray pushed it up the side of the crater and into the hands of Smith and Willard. I slid back a chunk of metal that was blocking several of the fuel valves when they busted into flames.

Agatha raced over and doused the ship with a blast of sand. Ray stopped pushing the fuel tank and through heavy breathing, said.

“Guys we can’t push this stuff across the entire planet. We’re going to need another way.”

Annabelle and Toni stepped inside the ship and were brainstormed ideas. I heard a low humming sound, and then a loud crash, and the door flew off. After several hours of crashing and cursing

They whizzed by on a hover cart they rigged up by attaching several seats to a platform along with a control panel and the large storage hold. They were able to rig it to float by attaching the former space suits manned maneuvering units to the bottom of the platform, creating a hovercraft. Annabelle and Toni spoke together.

“Everyone can ride and carry their stuff under two conditions, we get to be the pilots, and we get to name it the cosmic carriage.”

We filled the storage unit with everything we thought we could ever possibly use it to fix our ship. We almost gutted the rocket. I climbed into the seat behind Annabelle and James sat next to me, Toni and Agatha behind Gabriel and us, Willard and Smith flew above us as lookouts. Ray kept the Giant fuel tanks kinetic energy at max, which let it slide behind with ease.

James spoke up.

"Hey, I hate to sound like a jerk, shouldn't we have some protection from the rain and razor wind?"

Toni ran his fingers through his hair and stroked his goatee.

"You are right, so let's get some sides and a roof for this thing."

Ray, James, and I ripped some of the metal panels from the ship and attached them to the craft. I looked back and realized it looked like an old west carriage metal and with thrusters instead of wheels. We all climbed back inside and shut the doors. We began to speed off and traveled faster and faster.

"Hey Agatha, how far away is this lady, and what can we expect from her?"

Agatha's face turned red and angry, her eyebrows narrowing.

"Catalyst it's not going to be easy people will die I'm telling you right now, it's about ten clicks south of here she has a citadel. I have only been there once, I know there are guards one floor, monsters, demons, traps I will try to lead us through the best I can, it is going to be tough. Catalyst is possible that people are a prisoner there. She keeps people alive to feed on them …so we have to go face her."

I turned to Toni and Annabelle

"You heard her let's go! Once you see this citadel, stop, and we will finalize a plan."

I heard the low humming sound of James forging a weapon from the blood. I watched him as he formed another sickle-shaped weapon this time. It was more like a flat sickle sword. "That's it!" James screamed excitedly.

"This whole time, I've been trying to think of a signature weapon, and I finally found it. After I had served my final military tour, I was hired as a weapons archivist for several museums. I studied history's greatest weapons."

Toni smiled and said, "Dude, what a great choice the Kohpesh a favorite sword of the ancient Egyptians. They would execute their prisoners in large groups with the weapons also were able to disarm their opponents with ease. Agatha leaned forward.

"Guys shut up; we are approaching the citadel I suggest we take it in three teams of three. Gabriel and his guys can take it from the roof and work their way down. Catalyst you, James and Annabelle, take the ground floor and work your way up. Toni, Raymond, and I will take on the guards outside the castle. Everyone must work toward the middle. The Duchess of death sits on her threw at the center of the building," said Agatha.

The carriage came to a complete stop. For a moment, everyone was still, and it was quiet. We got out of the cosmic carriage. I was taking short quick steps to minimize noise and then. *Crack!* I looked over, and James had stepped onto a branch.

We all dove for the ground; it was too late she had seen us.

"Run now, stick to the plan," Agatha screamed.

The citadel was carved into the mountain side — hundreds of feet in the air and dozens of feet across. Several openings ran up the side, some natural and some human-made the craziest part of it all was that the moat that ran around the foot of it was the black acid. A great door of stone opened at the foot of the castle, and a man rode Out on the back of a small Dinosaur like a beast. He began to speak, and then I realized it was the man from the video, the captain of *the Orion.*

"Surrender now trespassers, and you will suffer only slightly. My queen has a proposition for you. She will let one of you live if you do what she says. It can either be chosen by her, or you can kill each other, and the last one standing shall live to tell the tale."

He stepped away and sat on his animal smug and satisfied ... I leaped at him and grabbed his throat, and injected box jellyfish toxin into his skin. I looked deep into his eyes.

"I have a counter-proposal, tell your master that Catalyst killed you and that I am coming for her, and I will kill everyone inside unless she releases whatever prisoners she has. We will take any supplies she may have. You better hurry I gave you enough poison to kill you in five excruciating minutes"

The man screams pierced my ears as he retreated into the castle.

"Dude, what the hell? Why did you kill that man? That's dark, even for you!" Toni said.

I walked toward the castle when I grabbed my swords and slid the blade between my hands and coated it in stonefish poison. I looked at Annabelle and then at Toni.

"You don't stay alive by letting others do the same. If I didn't kill him, he would have surely killed me. We cannot take it easy on them. We are playing to live, and we are playing for keeps. I swung my sword through the air and raised my blade to the sky. "New plan," I shouted.

"We walk in the door, and we kill anyone who even looks like they're going to attack us, and when we get to the Duchess, I kill her myself now, Charge!"

We marched into the building with weapons drawn and ready. The lights were dim, and I felt warmth in the air. Suddenly, I heard the stomping of claws on concrete. A dinosaur-like beast burst forth through the wall. He jumped and landed on Smith and knocked him to the floor and sunk his teeth into Smiths' wing. Toni swung his hand. Underhand and his sword into the beast side. Purple blood seeped onto the floor. The acid moat bubbled and burst, raining drops of acid and mud over everyone and everything.

The alien Dinosaurs burst from the building. At least a dozen or so. James slid his sickle sword through the stomach of one. Another bit him on his thigh. He grabbed the mouth and ripped the beast clean in half. Gabriel and Willard shot into the sky. Annabelle and Raymond drew their swords.

Ray would take away their kinetic energy as he ran. They stopped in their tracks, and Annabelle sliced them up. The dinosaurs charged at our teeth and claws flaring.

Gabriel, Willard, and Smith. Flew into the air and all at once they breathed acid from their mouths. They formed a solid ring around the aliens and trapped them inside the wall of bubbling acid.

"James, throw me!" I screamed.

He lifted me and tossed me into the ring of monsters. I slashed several of the dinosaurs and filled them with the poison of the stonefish. Some of their hearts stopped, and they dropped dead, and others seized and then died. Another beast leaped onto my back and knocked me to the floor.

He tried to sink his teeth into my neck. The beast blood began to drip on my face; he let out a scream and fell on me dead. A loud *sssssssshuck* and a sword pulled out of his body. An arm pulled me to my feet and saw it was Annabelle. I smiled at her.

"Thanks for saving my life! I guess that means we are even." Annabelle opened her lips to respond when the Duchess interrupted her.

"You have faced the pets you are no match for the master, I am power, true power I can kill you any way I wish I can control the causes of death at will and I will kill you so slowly. You know people are interested at first, they will say anything to try to live. To try to convince you to save them. In the end, everyone begs for a quick death. You Catalyst shall be no exception as I promised I would kill you last."

It was then I felt the heat from the acid rise, and then the Duchess of death stepped out of the acid without a blemish. As If it were only water. She had only taken one step when she grabbed Smiths' ankle from the sky. She filled his legs with worms, and they ate him alive. His screams could be heard for miles. "NOOOOOOOOOO!" Willard, and Gabriel shouted.

The Duchess went from man to woman and killed e single one of Agatha's crew differently.

The Duchess reached for Agatha and grabbed her arm. Ray looked over and screamed.

"No, I won't let you kill her. He tried to take away her kinetic energy; he couldn't. The Duchess turned to Ray and blasted him. At first, we thought she hadn't tried to kill him, she had. She was killing him by making him lose his sanity.

Ray raised his hand into the air and began siphoning Off all our kinetic energy.

"Watch this, my deceived and distraught friends."

He grabbed a sword and used our combined kinetic energy to achieve super speed. He raced next to me and slid the sword into my side, and I fell to my knees weak. He kicked James in the chest and ran up His body, jumping into the air and cut Willard's wings off. Raymond walked toward Annabelle and drew his sword. "NOOOOOOO, I jumped to my feet and grabbed Ray by his hair, pushing poison into the roots of his scalp, and he fell to the floor in cardiac arrest. The Duchess of death was not done; she grabbed Willard by his arms; she ate a few of his fingers. I saw James, Toni, and Gabriel try to attack it was if she could slow them down without even touching them. She dismembered the last of Agatha's crew members while also irradiated him.

"Demon no more, we shall do whatever you ask. Spare the rest of my friends these gruesome deaths. The Duchess stopped and turned to me. She turned a solid shade of black with crimson-colored eyes.

"I will melt the skin from your bones and boil the blood from your veins before I let any of you go. You are my feast. Your so-called friend Agatha brought you to me as a sacrifice so that she could live."

Toni drew his bone sword and swung it at the demon woman. She grabbed his leg and began to fill it with radiation. His leg bubbled and burst. Toni spun his sword and chopped off his leg. His blood oozed over the floor. Before the Duchess could kill Toni, James leaped over and Hardened the blood on Toni's leg stump. Annabelle and Agatha grabbed their swords and stepped next to me.

Agatha said, "Catalyst, I told you I wouldn't betray you, and I haven't. I brought you here because she can be killed; she's not immortal."

I looked at her and Annabelle. I nodded and smiled. Annabelle said.

"Catalyst, you can do this; kill her. We will find a fuel source and escape the planet."

She kissed my cheek and squeezed my hand.

"Agatha, I know I can, not alone," I said.

The Duchess moved over to where James was standing.

"Be silent, here's a new deal I let you live if you kill Your best friend or your girlfriend."

She reached into the acid lake and pulled out monsters made of the acid, and the grabbed James and Annabelle. I heard their skins burn and sizzle. I looked at the faces of my best friend and the girl I had grown to become so close to. I looked at Agatha and Toni.

"Gabriel now!" I shouted

Agatha tossed me James's sickle sword from the ground, and Toni tossed me his bone sword. I laced both with cobra venom spit. Gabriel flew down and picked me up with his claws and flew me through the air. He stopped and tossed me right above the Duchess of death. I stabbed the sickle sword into her throat, and the other I slid across her arm. She flayed and grabbed at James and me. I Pulled the swords until they met, leaving an open wound as she fell to her knees. Her body was fighting the poison hard, trying to heal itself.

Gabriel flew down and spat acid onto the acid monsters and then retracted the ooze back into his body, monsters, and all.

James raced over to me and grabbed my hand. Together we plunged our hands into the Duchess's open wounds, and I pumped her body full of Taipan snake poison. James stuck his hand into her blood and hardened her blood. She fell to the ground like a busted statue. James and I collapsed from exhaustion from extreme use of our powers, which caused me to blackout.

Chapter seven

The razor wind cut deep into my flesh; blood ran down my forehead like beads of sweat. My eyes had trouble opening and adjusting to the light. I stood to my feet, and my spine popped.

"Catalyst, are you ok!" Annabelle asked when she ran over to me. Her and Toni tended to the wounds of everyone else. She helped me walk and kissed my cheek. I smiled and gave her a tight hug. I looked over at James, whose arm was still bleeding. Toni wrapped the wound. Annabelle helped me walk over, and I sat next to them.

"Toni, thank you for giving aide to the rest of us; you should tend to your leg," Said James.

James and I helped him into the carriage; The rest of us climbed inside. We took a moment of silence for the people we lost. Toni and Annabelle drove toward the Citadel. The low hum of the thrusters was the only sound to break the silence.

Gabriel, the man who a few days, before I wish, would shut his mouth, sat their head down, and his jaw tightly clenched. Ever since he lost his friends at the hand of the Duchess, he hadn't said a word.

"Gabriel, are you going to be ok? I know they meant a lot to you. More than any of us will ever know. From what we could tell they were good men, and they saved our lives, and for that, we are grateful, "I said.

Gabriel raised his head, and through his Ink, colored tears screamed.

"When we were eleven, Willard, Smith, and I was kidnapped and beaten every day. Until we would do whatever he told us to do. The man who kidnapped us wanted us to rob him. One day we went to steal documents from a business and got caught. I got caught. When our boss got hold of us. I started to tell him that it was my fault and mine alone. Smith and Willard interrupted me and told him that it was all our fault. He beat us to death, or at least that's what the doctors and medical examiners thought. We were only in a coma and awoke to our bodies rotting and the strontium-90 eating away at our bone marrow. After all their doings they tried to kill us for years and when they couldn't they sent us to this planet to cover up their mistakes. For years we lived on this planet fighting and surviving. Until, of course, we met your bunch of merry men, and we know you for a few days, and now they're dead!

I promise when this is all over Catalyst, I will kill everyone that you love."

I looked over at him and grabbed him by the shoulder, and I looked through his eyes and into his soul.

"I am sorry killing them will not bring back the ones you lost. They would want you to finish the mission and get the better life that you all wanted, and after all this, if you still want to kill my family, then I promise I will kill you with the slowest and most painful poison I possibly can ."

Gabriel peered up at me.

"Not if I kill you first by drowning you with acid until it eats away at your bones."

I extend my hand.

"It's a deal then whenever we get back to Earth. It's E man for himself, and the winner gets the ultimate prize. He gets to keep his life."

The *Cosmic carriage* rattled as it passed over the bridge that spanned the moat. James looked around before he spoke; his loud voice echoed off the walls.

"This place would be one hell of a fortress or like a base. Let's check this place out! Dibs on the big room!"

I turned around, and Annabelle slid her hand into mine.

"Come on Catalyst, we better keep up with him — Agatha, who had also been quiet spoke.

"let's not forget why we are here. Save any prisoners she may have had and search for a fuel source for the ship."

We walked into the dark citadel, Items from people who died before us lay strewn throughout. None of them seemed like they could have helped us get off the planet. A crazy bright light blinded me.

With the light came to immense heat, and then I felt the smoke fill my nostrils.

I fell to the floor, and the other bodies did the same. I clawed at the ground to get up; I couldn't force myself too. I heard a sudden low swishing sound like the sound air brakes make. I awoke to cell door slamming shut, surrounded solid walls — no seams or bolts or anything anywhere.

As if I were inside a perfect cube. I raised my hands to my face; my hands were fastened together in a solid metal sphere. I sat down to think about how I could escape when a voice began to emit from the ceiling. A screen blinked on and a man who appeared to be a grey and scaly raptor-like alien. His grey head was covered only with a red double crest. He was Similar to the dinosaurs that Duchess of death controlled before. He began to laugh and speak.

"Humans are so foolish. They think everything is as simple as Earthly entertainment. That if you kill the leader, all the others who follow her will go away. No, we are still here and will use you and your knowledge and some of you we will eat. Get comfortable and acquainted with your roommates because you're never leaving."

The screen clicked off. From the shadows of my cell stepped a man. His skin was wrinkled his hair short and grey; His eyes were dark, his skin bronze.

"Allow me to introduce myself; my name is Museum Master. You may call me Zadok. I, too, am from Earth. Many years ago, at least several decades ago, my crew and I were the first ships ever sent to this planet by the United Nations. We were told it was to see if the planet was Habitable in case of Nuclear destruction of the Earth. That was only partially true. They wanted a place that they could dump all their experiments and mistakes away from the public eye. Before they cut communication with us, they told us that our lives being spent on this planet and never coming home was justifiable.

"Since that day, they have sent dozens of ships here, most of which have long been dead. As I am sure you have come to realize that a great many people are not. Including the beast which resembled dinosaurs that were created when the United Nations attempted to use the traits of Dinosaurs to give humans super abilities. It worked too well; it gave them dinosaur abilities alright along with dinosaur-like bodies. That demon only left me alive to do her bidding. You see my ancestors were guardians of temples in Egypt. The guardians of relics and tombs, artifacts, and museums. Throughout time in e civilization, my bloodline had craved these things. My father spent his life creating a device, a medallion that only members of my bloodline can use. It can pull in artifacts or relics; especially weapons from Time for a limited time. What about you, sir? What's your story, "Zadok said.

I spoke with hesitation because I did not trust this new man.

"My name is Catalyst, I can control, and poison and toxins, I will only tell you what you want to hear if you promise to help break out."

He nodded in agreement, and I told him the origin of my powers

" A long time ago when I was only about five my birth father was killed in a bank robbery, my mother was offered a high paying job out of state, he didn't want to take me, so she sent me to live with my aunt, uncles, and cousins. One night my cousins were playing outside; they were killed by a king cobra.

The first thing my uncle said to me was, why couldn't. I have been the one to die. For five years, he took me to this laboratory to inject me with e venom, poison, and toxin known to man after it would almost kill me; he would give me the anti-venom. He would beat me and let other professors test their experiments on me. One fateful day all the poisons and toxins from my body mixed with a mystery drug. Next thing I know, I accidentally poison my dog, and I realized I had the power to poison So I did what anyone would do. I used it to get revenge on my uncle, and I killed him with the cruelest poison. Then I did the same with the people who killed my father. I hunted them down one by one until they were all dead."

Zadok stared at me with his mouth agape. Fear flooded his eyes.

"Well my friend, that's rather dark on that note, what is your master plan. I've been here for almost a hundred years, yet I am still here."

I stood up and stared into the corner of the room before speaking.

"You never had Toni or me. Toni's superpower is that he has an impeccable recall of e battle in history, E strategy. I assume I would include prison breaks of sorts."

Zadok laughed and grabbed his stomach as he bent over.

"My family were keepers of time. We guard the history of the world. It's what ties me to all of these relics, yet you say this man can do better than I, please try."

Hmm, I stroked my chin and pondered the infinite possibilities and pitfalls. How can I get these dim-witted dinosaurs to open the door and let me talk to Toni? I banged on the walls until my knuckles bled. The door raised, and through it, one of the head dinosaurs entered. He spoke with a dramatic lisp, which made understanding him all the harder.

"Listen, Catalyst is it, your friends have told us so much about you.

Especially the pretty one, what was her name? Oh yes, Annabelle, if I remember right."

More dinosaurs filled the room and pinned me to the wall. They dug their claws into my shoulder.

"NO, don't you touch her, or I will kill you! "I screamed.

"Ah, you are in to position to make demands, my friend. You are mistaken. The Duchess of death did not keep you alive to feed on you. I kept you alive because each of you contained the power I wanted. With your Powers, I will conquer this planet, and I will use your friend to Fix my ship, and then I will conquer Earth."

I broke free of their grasp, and I punched the dinosaur in his long thin face with the shackle sphere. He started to laugh.

"My name is Ehud; I will be your downfall. He started to walk out of the room when I shouted after him.

"Let me tend to Toni's legs; he has lost a lot of blood and needs a new leg; he's no good to you dead. Ehud thought for a moment and then agreed he let Toni come in and brought in some equipment and tools.

"Toni, how's she doing?"

He looked at me with sadness in his eyes.

"She is alive, they broke her, and she's weak."

"Well then we have to get out of here, we have to save them we have to escape. Give me some ideas."

Toni's eyes glazed over; his mind flew through history. He spoke fast and, his words slurred as he spits of a list.

"During the United States Civil, there was a Confederate General named John Morgan. With his fellow prisoners, they burrowed under their prison in Ohio, and into ventilation shafts, they succeeded in their escape. In 1943, Oliver Philpot and two others escaped a German Pow camp, with a tunnel a wooden horse and fake papers, escape successfully. During "The great escape" Two hundred men escaped from several tunnels at a POW camp. However out of the initial two hundred only three escaped."

His rambling stopped, and he began to speak again.

"Catalyst most prisoners of war escape through tunnels or are rescued from the outside. We are being held in the mountain and not on the ground floor, what are we to do?"

The dinosaur men returned to grab Toni; I secured his new fake metal leg It fastened to his knee. It was more Like a pirate peg leg then a prosthetic foot. The dinosaur men refastened the metal sphere around my hands, ensuring I could not use them.

"Toni, I will save us. I will get us out of here! You have my word." I said

They dragged him out of the room, and the door hissed shut. I heard the screams of my friends even though they think of metal walls.

"Dude, you said you would help us now help. How do we break out of here?" I asked Zadok.

He turned to me, annoyed, and spoke dismissively.

"What can you not comprehend, we cannot escape. Even if we managed to escape, we would get recaptured or killed, and if we eluded That, we would run into another beast or probably a Villain. Some people's livestock. No matter what they do or go, no matter how much they try or do. They find only heartbreak and failure, and guess what, when you find success; it is only the prologue to further misfortune. A placeholder until the next problem. Some people never find their happy endings. If they did, people wouldn't know that their ending is happy. We cannot escape. I learned that a long time ago. It's time you do the same. He laid on the floor, in the corner like a dog. I sat down near him. My jaw clenched so tight it began to hurt.

"No. No, that is a narrow-minded view, and I won't accept it. You know what you are, a crazy older man. I would endure a life of endless ups, and downs battle after battle after battle to spend what little time I could with my friends and family and Annabelle. Sometimes you must enjoy whatever calms you can because life is a storm, and another will come that does not mean you close your sails in this doldrum that you have accepted. A Fate I hope never to accept. I will figure out a plan."

The door opened, and Ehud entered looking more human then dinosaur.

"Catalyst, I have broken the will of your friends, and now I shall break yours. Tell me what your limits are, tell me what your weaknesses are, and tell me how to leave this planet." Said Ehud.

I spit in his face, laughed as it slid down his grey face.

"You find these childish acts amusing you won't for long if you notice I am in a more human state. This is compliments of the girl Agatha. I took her blood and absorbed it in my bloodstream. It healed some of the dinosaur's mutated blood. I see the shock on your face mister Catalyst. I barely believed it myself at first, yet it is true." Said Ehud.

"Don't you touch her or any of my friends or so help me, I will kill you."

He walked over to me and dug his claws into my back, ripping off a hand full of bloody flesh.

“AHAHAHAHAH I WON’T TALK,” I screamed through clenched teeth. Blood pooled at my feet, and pain seared through my spine. Ehud looked at me and smiled maniacally. He grabbed a metal bar and heated it.

“What are your weaknesses, young one,” Ehud asked.

I closed my mouth and held it tight. Knowing that I could not tell him anything. He dragged the hot metal bar across my shoulder blades I screamed, and I heard my flesh sizzling and popping as if being cooked. Still I said nothing. If I talked, then he would no longer need my friends or us. We would never get home.

“Bring in Agatha and the blood drawing equipment,” Said Ehud.

I looked over at Zadok, who sat in the corner as if nothing were happening. Still, Quiet, and unmoving. Agatha was shoved through the door. She looked weak, grey her, with her mouth gagged. Her eyes are wide. Ehud raised the metal pole again as if to strike my back, except he used it to burn Agatha and knock her to her knees.

“NO! No more!” I screamed.” I will tell you what you want to hear. My weakness is poison. I can control most earthly animal poisons; yes, the alien poison would be enough to kill me.” Ehud smiled and laughed.

“You lie mister Catalyst, your friend James told us if we introduce new poison to your blood, you will be able to control it henceforth. Your weakness is your feelings; he grabbed the rod and swung it at Agatha. He brought the pipe down on her shoulder. Sending her sprawling to the floor. “NO!” I screamed Again.

I tried to break free of my wall restraints.

"Catalyst you will not try to help her either, no first aid will be administered thanks to your visit with Toni. I know you cannot go five minutes without planning an escape. I promise you; you will not be tunneling out I have guards on the base of the mountain. They patrol the skies and even underground. There is no escape for you." Said Ehud.

The men carried Agatha out as if to tease me even more. I pulled on the restraints again until I fell to my knees weak. Ehud laughed a deep and hearty evil laugh.

"You are breaking already. Imagine what will happen when we bring in the woman you love."

He walked out of the door and chucked a hunk of bread onto the floor along with a bowl of purple water.

"All that I want from you Catalyst is for you to serve me. Your powers will be most useful when I try to conquer earth. You can either use them for me while you are living, or I will figure out how to take them from you and then kill you. The door slammed shut behind him, and I screamed and fell to floor, the pain covering my entire body. I fell to the floor in a puddle of my blood, and I slipped into sleep, craving for any nightmare that would be better than the one I was living.

Chapter Eight

"Zadok wakes up," I whispered.

He rolled over to stare at me. His finger perched in front of his lips.

"Mr. Catalyst, would you please be quiet. It is the middle of the night, and I will not get beaten for you."

I crawled over to where he was laying and sat next to him.

"I know what you said before; I have a plan. My friend James is also being held prisoner here. Ehud Locked my hands, and he Took away Toni's sword as well as the rest of our weapons. Except James is his Arsenal. You see, he can make weapons from his blood. So, I suggest we get to James so he can make us weapons, and then instead of tunneling out or anything they expect we will kill all these guys and walk right out the front door. What do you think? Will you help us?"

Zadok thought for a moment. His breathing was heavy as he muttered to himself. He stood up and paced the room from wall to wall. He stopped and stuck out his hand. I shook it hesitantly and cracked a half-smile. Zadok cracked a sly smirk.

“Congratulations Mr. Catalyst, that is officially the worst idea I have ever heard.”

I let go of his hand and shoved him back. If he weren’t going to help me, I would do it myself. How would I get them to open the door? They only open the door to throw in the scraps off food, and I can’t attack them because they bring an entire troop. Then an idea had occurred to me. The next time Ehud would come to interrogate me, I would tempt him with what he wanted most.

Blood and lots of it. Hours went by, and then days. I couldn’t take it anymore. Why was he not coming to interrogate me and torture me? The longer I stayed there, the more chance of my friends being hurt was. I drove myself insane. I could not take the waiting and uncertainty anymore. If Ehud did not come, I would make him come in.

I walked over to Zadok and looked him in the eyes.

“I’m sorry, I have to save my friends. If they kept, you alive this long, they must need you for something, and if they need you, they will save you.”

Zadok looked worried and feared consumed his face. I beat him with the sphere cuffs. I hit him again and again and again. Blood seeped everywhere. At first, he screamed until suddenly, he fell silent, and I stopped for fear of killing him. There was so much blood it completely covered my cuffs and dropped onto my arms.

The door opened, and Ehud was standing there in the half-human form. He entered the room and reached into the pool of blood and absorbed it through his skin. Right before my eyes, I saw Ehud turn back into a Human.

"Restrain him! ", Ehud Shouted to his henchmen.

They attached my sphere to the wall. I saw Zadok's fresh blood still caked to my cuffs. Ehud placed his fingers together and paced the floor.

"You see Catalyst; you are a villain. People have this belief that everyone is good that's a lie. Everyone is a villain. Deep down all it takes to let this villain out is the right incentive or circumstance. Take yourself, for instance, a few days without seeing your friends, especially your love interest, and next thing you know, your beating this random guy to death. He didn't help you escape; you justified it by saying you are doing it to try and save your friends.

Guess what everyone justifies their actions. Everyone is the hero of their own life story.

"Me, I accept that I am the villain. Your friends have blood. I want it. You and your friends have powers, and I want them. You're a villain now, and I will make you prove it," Said Ehud.

The cell door opened James and Agatha were pushed inside and then shoved to their knees.

"I will give you a choice, hero. Save your best friend or the one you think you love. The other I will take their blood and drain it from them as you writhe and watch."

Zadok turned away from us. The dinosaur-men dug their claws into James and Annabelle. James screamed.

"Catalyst save Annabelle, don't worry about me. I can handle myself."

Ehud started to laugh as he unhooked my sphere from the wall and dragged me in front of my friends.

"Kill one of them, or I will slay them both."

I hesitantly shuffled over to Annabelle and kissed her cheek. She jerked her face away,

"Annabelle I will get us all out of this I promise "

James and I locked eyes and nodded at each other. I lifted the sphere and bashed it into James' chest. Annabelle started to scream and cry. I hit the sphere against James' chest again. His blood splattered to the floor. I kneeled to catch my breath. Then I propped myself up with my elbows. James slumped to the floor in his blood. Ehud walked over

"I said, give me your blood."

He reached his hand up and began to absorb the blood from the floor.

"You wanted blood. You can have it," I said.

The blood turned into darts then shot through the air. They pierced Ehud's body all over.

"Ha-ha, you think a few little spikes will hurt me?"

He grabbed his chest and fell to the floor. The tree Frog's poison has reached his heart.

James cuffs burst open, and he held a handful of Knives.

"Catalyst catches!" Said, James.

The dinosaur-men grabbed Annabelle and lunged for me. I clasped my hands around the knives and cocked my hand back.

"Annabelle duck, don't flinch."

I chucked a knife into the face of the dinosaur-man that was holding Annabelle. He fell, and She wriggled free. James tossed her a knife, and she turned and stabbed the men around James.

I dropped my voice to a whisper.

"Annabelle lower the door, don't close it, we need to make a plan, and James is weak from the loss of blood.

Also, this new shmuck is named Zadok, and he has info on this citadel. We need to rescue Toni, Agatha, and Gabriel. We must kill all these Dinosaur-men to fix our ship and go home.

Annabelle, I missed you so much," I said.

I pulled her close and hugged her tightly. She hugged me back then pulled away and looked at me in a way she never had before

"Thank you for helping to rescue us, what did it cost you? You almost killed an innocent man, Catalyst. That's not you. You're supposed to have changed. You're supposed to be becoming a Hero. Heroes don't hurt people for their gain. I don't know if I can be close to you anymore."

She walked over and sat next to Zadok, introducing herself and making small talk. I sat next to James, and I began thinking of ways to get out of the building with all my friends and not letting any of them get hurt.

"She'll come back around dude give her some time. Give me a few minutes, and then we'll figure out how to get out of here. We have to bring this guy?" James asked.

I looked from Zadok to Annabelle and then back at James.

"We have to I almost killed him, and besides, it's what a hero would do, plus he could be helpful he has a cool power."

We busted Zadok's sphere cuffs, and then we headed out the door. James formed his favorite blood sickle sword. His knuckles clenched around the blade.

"We should hit Ehud's office first I am sure that's where your weapons will be, and then your friends will be locked in rooms close by. The hard part will be fighting hundreds of dinosaur-men down a hundred stories." Said Zadok

"Well, we better get started then," Annabelle said as she pushed past us and out of the door.

We entered a dimly lit hallway, the ceiling hung low, bugs covered the ground, and moss caked the walls. Zadok led the way with Annabelle close behind. He made a quick turn, and in front of us stood a large archway. It was Ehud's room and arsenal as well as the hold for his treasure and souvenirs. There were several dinosaur – men who stood guard. Before they could scream or flee or even attack, James had already killed a few of them, and I poisoned the rest.

We entered his sanctuary; the room was lavish with a burst of gold and purple color and trim. Along each wall from top to bottom sat rows of shelves on each shelf sat several relics. In the center of the room were Toni's bone sword and Zadok's amulet. Zadok grabbed the amulet and put it around his neck. His eyes flickered gold and then returned to brown. I grabbed Toni's sword. We began to walk out the door when James turned to me.

"Catalyst, you sure you don't want to take any of these other weapons. There are dozens here."

I took a quick look around at the plethora of trinkets and treasures. A long time ago, a wise man once told me greed would never satisfy you; it will always destroy you.

"Annabelle, you take a weapon you want. The rest will stay here; taking them will only slow us down."

Annabelle looked at all the weapons; she took her time and studied the uses of each one. She reached for a circular one. It was a perfect metal black disk.

Zadok said, “That is an ancient Chakram they are throwing weapons like ninja stars the chakram is larger and can also be used hand to hand. After we rescue your friends, I can train you on how to use them.”

She hugged Zadok tightly and tossed her arms around his neck.

“Let’s go rescue Toni first, he is the best fighter and our strategist,” I said.

Zadok looked at Annabelle and smirked his stupid smirk.

“I don’t think so; I think we should rescue that dragon guy first, once you take the muzzle off his acid can set us free.”

I looked at him and ran my fingers through my long hair. How would he know about Gabriel and his powers unless Annabelle told him? They only talked for a few minutes. I doubt she would have told him.

“Well, Mr. Museum Master last I checked I was the boss, and I say we should spring Toni first.”

Zadok stepped up to me and squared up his shoulders and clenched his jaw.

“You might not trust me; you might not like me. You know I am right and that you cannot doubt me. Plus, you said it yourself. I have been here the longest. I would know the citadel best. Now, if you follow me, I will take us to the Dragon man’s cell.” Said Zadok.

We left Ehud's room and descended the building. We peaked into the next floor down were about twenty dinosaur men stood guard.

"Catalyst should we kill them or try to knock them out; heroes are supposed to try and not kill people, right?" James asked.

Zadok's eyes glowed goldenly, and through his amulet he pulled a Katana.

"They are not people. They are beast that only knows how to kill, and we must kill them before they kill us."

He sliced through dinosaur after dinosaur; the first few were taken by surprise. The next jumped upon him. His sword crashed to the floor. They lowered their teeth to Zadok's neck, saliva dripped down his neck. When Annabelle dove through the air and embedded her chakram into the dinosaurs back, he fell to the ground and flailed about before dying. James cut his palm once again and was quick to make throwing stars and sent them into the dinosaur's necks and killed them. After all the enemies were dead, we opened the door.

The first thing I saw was Gabriel. His arms were wrapped around Agatha, and they were talking as if they were not in a solid metal room built to make you go insane.

"Agatha? Out of all the people in this world, in any world. Did you go with Gabriel? His skin feels like a gator."

She looked up at Gabriel and back at me before responding.

"We have been here for weeks. It was either talk with him or stare into the corner and go nuts. So, we took the opportunity to get to know each other better. Underneath his tough warped exterior Is an interesting and genuinely good guy. Catalyst doesn't act like you're the good guy I had only know you a few days when you let everyone, I know, die. Thanks for the rescue, though".

She gave me a dirty look and turned away.

James helped Agatha and Gabriel to their feet. Zadok broke the muzzle off Gabriel's face. The group had grown quiet as we exited the room and walked down to the next floor.

"Is this the room Toni is being held in?" I asked Zadok.

He looked at the door and then back at me before responding.

"Yes, the one you call Toni and another."

I had begun to look at Zadok. I opened my mouth to speak when James and Gabriel had already begun to force the door of the cell off the track. The door let out a loud hiss. We entered the room, and I cut the rest of the door away with Toni's sword.

"You won't torture me this time; I will kill you first." Someone screamed from above us.

Toni leaped down upon us from the ceiling. He shoved his metal leg into my shoulder.

"This time I'll kill you first, I spent days sharpening my leg to a point."

He pushed his spike leg farther into my shoulder; blood gushed from my shoulder. Gabriel and Zadok pulled him off me, and James touched my shoulder, infusing his blood into my shoulder and coagulating the wound.

"Toni, calm down. We are your friends! Ehud is dead. We killed him. Now it's time to go," said Agatha.

Toni tried to keep fighting us. Gabriel spits onto the floor and melted metal. We wrapped the metal around one of Toni's wrist and pinned him to the floor.

"We don't have time for this; we need to keep him restrained and go before darkness rises once again." Said Gabriel.

James grabbed Toni and slammed him back to the floor. I had to knock him unconscious.

"Hey Catalyst, who is that? "Annabelle asked.

A man emerged from the corner. He laid his hand on Toni did not say a word. So, Gabriel made him a pair of cuffs too. We continued to descend to the lower levels of the citadel, more mysteries arising with each room we explored. We entered a room with a low hanging ceiling. Beakers covered the tables, and blueprints strewn over the walls. The blueprints were plans to build a ship. Toni was coming to and muttered to himself.

"Reuben, Catalyst, Raymond," he snapped out of the trance and reverted to sanity. "Agatha! Catalyst, James, we made out?"

I took Toni's Sword and cut through the cuffs. I handed him back his sword and shook his hand and gave him a quick hug. He shoved me aside.

"Toni, it's good to have you back, man," I said.

Chapter Nine

Reuben was a man of few words. The only reason we even knew his name was because once Toni regained control of his mind, and wasn't delusional anymore, he explained who the mysterious cellmate of his was. From what I understood, Reuben could change the state of matter of things by merely touching them. According to Toni, Reuben is so quiet that in two weeks, the most information he could get out of him was that his name is Reuben, he is only 17, and he misses his girlfriend.

Most of the crew had gone to bed for the night, Agatha and Zadok were on guard duty and made sure that the part of the citadel with the lab was locked down. Toni, Annabelle, and I tried to figure out a plan on how to use the blueprints along with the ship parts from the Orion to fix the *Mach Infinity*. If the parts were where we left them, that is.

We spent half the night combining ideas from various ships and utilizing the best parts of every ship. If we messed up, we would be dead and all that messed up stuff the president of the NAC and the nations of the world had done for hundreds of years. Would go unpunished. I couldn't let that happen.

Toni waved me over to talk to me away from Agatha.

"First man, I want to say thank you for rescuing all of us. I don't know how you did it, and I don't know if I want To. I especially am grateful for getting my sword back. I was able to craft a new leg with that Zadok guy's help. Catalyst, I don't know how far any of us are going to get if you and Annabelle don't fix whatever is going on between you two. Trust me, man, throughout history, people always lose battles when they're distracted by relationships and quarrels among their lover. Fix it before it cost us a battle or worse someone's life," said Toni

"Toni she won't talk to me if I force her to talk, she might never like me again, now what do you know about this Reuben guy?"

Toni ran his hand through his goatee before responding.

"Catalyst e time I try to talk about relationships or other things besides adversaries or ways to get home you ask a question to get us back on this greater mission. I know how important it is for you to get home. I don't know why. You have no family. You are fueled by your need to be needed and to have a mission.

If we fight all the beast on this planet, all we will get out of it is that we get "home "A place that hates us and then we will get to fight more. Ehud was right. Another evil will always rise. Even if that evil spurs from those close to you.

You need to talk. When I was in my cell, I couldn't talk. I stopped myself from talking to him. Reuben barely speaks. I talk, and he listens. Reuben's is like the younger brother I never got to have. Without words, we are nothing. You need to start talking about more than your story," said Toni.

Toni stopped rambling, and his eyes wandered to where Reuben laid. He stood up and grabbed the blanket that laid at Reuben's feet. Toni pulled the blanket to Reuben's chin and sat down.

I stood shocked at everything Toni had been talking about. How he talked to fast and jumped subject's I couldn't get a word in. Ehud had played such a small part in our lives; he had affected us so much. Toni mentally. Agatha physically. She had become so weak from having her blood drained; she could no longer use her powers. I knew I could get us home, at what cost.

James walked into the room and placed his hand on my shoulder. He shook his head.

"Man, you're tired. You're exhausted, and you're letting Toni get to you. Now get some sleep. We can plan the ship tomorrow,", said James.

I nodded and gave him a half hug. I was too tired to argue too tired to speak. I laid down and fell asleep to the familiar sound of Annabelle dragging her pen across paper.

Several hours later, I awoke to the sound of footsteps a few feet away. I peeked over the edge of the table where I was lying. I could barely see Zadok in the center of the room. He was scribbling in the same fashion as the writing on the walls.

I knew I couldn't trust him. No wonder he did not want us to escape. No wonder he wanted to push us apart. He even succeeded at splitting up Annabelle and me. I began to stand when I saw him pull out a sketch of me. He flipped it over, and on the back was a list of my powers. He flipped through the entire stack, including every single one of my friends. Then it hit me. I realized what Toni Said was wrong. I did have many reasons for why I wanted to get home.

My friends deserve a good place to live instead of this awful place. Yes, it is going to be an uphill battle; in the end, we could be free. We have the power to stand up to the evil forces of the government and everyone else. How's that old saying go?

"All it takes for evil to succeed is for good men to do nothing."

So that's it we will do something. I must do whatever it takes to save Earth and the people. Let freewill rule the world again. Bring peace and prosperity to the people. If I fail, it will mean my head and my friends and a global dystopian government that will kill anyone they want.

My focus snapped back, and I looked at Zadok again. I rose to my feet and heard the soot crackled underfoot.

"Zadok! I screamed"

"How much of this were you behind? Was it all of it? You've been studying us watching us. You know our powers. Maybe even our weaknesses. Is this why you didn't want me to help you escape?"

My fist connected with the older man's face.

I stretched my fingers, thinking of what poison to use.

Zadok stepped back with a surprised look on his face. He tapped the pen against the sketches.

"Catalyst, I know you have been through a great deal; we all have. If Toni went insane because of Ehud, then you've become paranoid. I told you my back-story I told you the truth. I sat in the same cell as you for weeks, watching as they tortured you. I wanted to help; I could not. Your delusions are unfounded, and they have no bases. I am looking at documents that were here before I ever stepped foot into this room. I walked in here for the first time. Agatha and I were standing guard while you and Toni were in here. Now I promise I am on your side I want to get home as much as you I've been here for almost a hundred years now, I am going to retire for the night, "Said Zadok.

I did not believe him, and I did not trust him. Something Toni said had hit me. He claimed he had gotten the phrase a new evil will always rise from Ehud Zadok had said it too.

I sat there awhile. I was leaning against the wall for support and thought a thousand thoughts. Then I saw Annabelle a few feet away, and I began to walk toward her to apologize and explain myself and tell her how I missed her when Toni and Zadok pushed into the room in a frenzy.

They shoved the sketches and everything else onto the floor. Toni slid a blueprint onto the table that showed a NASA logo. It depicted various fuel diagrams. Each one listed everything that we still don't have: a fuel source, an oxidizer, fuel pumps, and a combustion chamber. I turned to Toni before I spoke, I stroked my chin as I always did when I was deep in thought.

"Toni, I don't get what are you trying to show me? We already knew that we need a fuel source and all this other stuff that you are trying to show me?" I asked.

Toni's eyes ventured to the other side of the room, where Reuben sat staring at the wall. His eyes looked blank and meaningless.

"Catalyst before we do this, I need you to know that because I don't think we should go back or through all this does not mean I won't help. I care about Reuben as if he was my brother. He needs a chance that his life can be more than this planet. Even the way Earth is now will be better for him than any day here. I will do everything in my power to get us home. To get Reuben home. If nothing else, then attempting this will give him hope. I won't go with you." Said, Toni

I looked into Toni's eyes, and I saw he was sincere.

"Toni, you should come with us ..."

I began to say when Toni cut me off. He pointed to the drawing. At the Fuel and oxidizers.

"The simplest liquid rocket fuel is to use liquid oxygen as an oxidizer and liquid hydrogen as a fuel, It sounds easy back in the day when they used it on a recurring bases the biggest dilemma was that there is a cryogenic process in order to turn the gases into a liquid in order to put them into a tank on the spaceship. That is a luxury that we do not have, "said Toni.

The three of us sat and thought for a great length of time. Then a spark lit inside my brain. That I was not a rocket scientist, and neither was Toni or Zadok. Four more people were sleeping outside the door. They could come up with ideas as good as the other, not rocket scientist and I. James, Annabelle, Reuben, and Agatha entered the room and sat across from me. They took turns examining the diagrams as well as the terms and the faces of each other. Annabelle began to scribble in her book. She set down her pen and stepped to her feet.

"We do not have a complicated machine due to this thing that turns oxygen or hydrogen from gas to liquid; we don't need one. Can't the new guy change the state of matter an item is in? Who needs a glorified freezer when he can change the state of something simply by touching it," said Annabelle?

We all looked at each other as if the idea was so simple, how could we have missed it. Then James stood up with his questions.

"Dude, is that not water? I think I remember reading about that once the problem is if you don't have the aluminum rocket boosters, you'd need an incredibly large tank to house the ignition of the liquid fuels, "said James.

He sat down, Agatha jumped up and blurted out.

“Unless we don’t need a tank at all, hear me out if this Reuben guy can change the state of matter such as a gas to a liquid while we constantly heat it then we don’t need a tank,” said Agatha

Zadok paced the room. He wrote diagrams and formulas on the walls and the papers. Reuben looked at Toni In a way that conveyed his worry and fear of failure.

“This whole group love fest and inclusion sessions are nice; it still does not change the fact that Reuben can only change the state of matter something is in. For example, he can change a chair into a liquefied chair. He cannot break down the elements of it or combine them, said Toni. Zadok slammed his fist against the wall, and his eyes glowed goldenly; from his Amulet, he pulled out a solid black ring with a green stripe down the middle, and it was covered in spikes. Almost like the ring James wore before he got his arm cut off.

“In the year 2090, when few people had abilities or gifts or Powers my father invented this ring. It does not grant powers it merely enhances the powers you have and your ability to use them. Letting you reach your full potential. The side effects are unknown though”, said Zadok

Toni was pissed and took a swing at Zadok, he dodged, and Toni fell to the floor.

“No, we will find another way! We are not putting Reuben in danger. What if the side effect is that he dies?” Said Toni.

Zadok and Toni shoved each other and punched each other. Toni drew his bone sword and placed the blade against Zadok’s cheek. The blade was so close to his face that a patch of his beard got cut off and fell to the floor.

"No, stop! Don't hurt him! I don't want you guys fighting anymore. I'll do it to give me a ring! Said Reuben. At first, we all stood there in shock because Reuben had broken his silence and we had never even heard his voice before.

Zadok tossed Rueben the ring, and he slid it onto his ring finger. The green line glowed as spikes retracted into Reuben's finger. He let out a scream and reached down and touched Annabelle's pen. It liquefied and turned into the individual elements. The water, oxygen, pigments of the ink, carbon, and various other elements. Reuben touched the liquid again, and it turned back into a pen.

"There is hydrogen and oxygen in the air, right?" I said right as I said it Reuben had already started to convert the gas elements of the air into their liquid state.

I fell to my knees and grabbed my throat. It felt like I was suffocating, and something had ripped the air from my lungs. Reuben let go, and the pair returned to normal.

"If he cannot use the elements in the air, where can he get the hydrogen and oxygen supply from then?" asked Toni.

No one answered. We were all tired and weak from the last couple of days and the last few weeks and from trying to figure out how to get Home. Zadok left the room and returned after a few minutes. I heard a loud thud, Zadok had thrown one of the dead dinosaur men onto the desk.

"Plenty of hydrogen and oxygen in the blood of these dead beast might as well put the bodies to good use."

Chapter Ten

The morning light bled into the room. It forced its way through cracks in the walls; it engulfed the dead bodies and reflected off their dinosaur scales.I had been taken aback at what Zadok had proposed. I looked at the dead body, one which I had killed myself. I stood up and completely covered the body with a sheet. James looked over at me and shook his head no. I stepped up to Zadok and stared into his soulless eyes. I slammed the palms of my hands down onto the table.

"Zadok, this is not right. This is evil and injustice, and I cannot allow it! We are supposed to be heroes. I am done being the bad guy, and I have been trying to right my wrongs. There is always another way, one that does not involve desecrating the dead," I screamed.

Zadok approached the table and uncovered the dead man. Reuben placed a hand on the man's forehead, and the other pointed at Zadok. Zadok threw a chunk of Flint up into the air and across his sword, which created an intense spark.

Reuben shot liquid hydrogen and oxygen at the flint until it sparked an explosive reaction and sent the flint through the wall of the citadel. An explosive BOOM rang through the room. Zadok cracked a sly smile, and he beamed with pride. The test pushed Zadok's insistence That using the bodies was the only way to go. The test solidified how horrible the act was. I looked at the table, and all that remained of the dinosaur man's body was a few scales and a pool of various elements.

Zadok patted Reuben's shoulder and stepped back from the table. "That Catalyst proves the necessity for using the bodies. It is perfectly justified. The bodies can either sit here and rot or they can be the power that sends us home. This does not make us evil. They are dead; they feel not, so I do not feel for them. You would have them believe that this is an atrocity.

That I am evil, I say the evil would be to force them to stay on the wasteland of a planet when there are means of escape. Let them decide; we will have a vote. Those who side with me and using the bodies standby be, and whoever wants to stay here for who knows how long looking for another can go side with Catalyst, Said Zadok.

James was the first to stand he walked over to me and formed a bloody knife. With which he cut his palm and my own. We slid our hands across each other and locked fingers. James nodded and grabbed my shoulder.

"Bro, you know I am always with you; I told you when we first started this that I would always back you up, and I will," said James.

Agatha ran her fingers through her long hair and picked up a sword from the floor and slipped it into a sheath on her back.

"Catalyst, I know you're trying to do the right thing here, I have to agree with Zadok. We have to do whatever it takes to get home, and I feel like he is not afraid to do whatever it takes, "said Agatha.

She turned around and walked over to Zadok. Dragging her fingers through the pool of elements from the table and dragging the black liquid across Zadok's face and beard as if it were war paint.

Gabriel lifted himself off the ground and said, "Catalyst as always, you are wrong. I see no reason not to use this resource that arose when we needed it most. It is a gift from the Gods, I've been here for years and years, and finally there is a means of escape. I see no reason to pass it up."

He floated over to where Agatha stood and landed next to her. He looked over at Zadok with a sideways glare and sighed until he turned away from Agatha.

One at a time, everyone picked aside; I couldn't help think that was one of those defining moments of my life. You know one of those moments that changes the course of your whole story and shapes events yet to come.

Annabelle took one last look back at Zadok, and of course, Agatha, she turned and stood behind James.

"Catalyst, I'm sorry I sided with Zadok earlier. I shouldn't have left you and James; we still need to talk later," said Annabelle.

Before she finished speaking, Toni had grabbed his bone sword and slammed it into the ground at Zadok's feet. I am splitting stone into two.

"I'm sorry Catalyst I have to do what's best for Reuben and what's best for Reuben is to get home as soon as possible and if that means sacrificing animals who don't even feel anything and waste away to nothing when they could be used to get us home," said Toni.

After he had joined Zadok, Reuben was not far behind him. He had become Toni's shadows as well as Toni's strive. Zadok and the other turned to walk out of the room. Toni dragged his bone blade through the dirt. Zadok stopped and turned toward me running a hand through his thick beard. "Catalyst, I know you want to be this hero, do what is right. That it will make amends for e bad thing you have ever done, it will not. I don't think there is such thing as heroes and villains. People who do what they think needs to be done. So, you say a hero would not use these dead bodies. Well I am no hero. Agatha Hugged Annabelle and James goodbye. Toni shook my hand; it was weird though. I had not gotten used to my left hand as my dominant hand. I glanced down at the burned and charred remnants of my right hand.

"Catalyst, we are going to collect the bodies I know you don't like it. It's what we are going to do. We'll be back in the morning, and then we will head back to the *Mach infinity*, and we will get them home, said Toni" he walked out the door, followed by Reuben, Zadok, Agatha, and Gabriel.

For the first time since we had been on this planet, I had no idea what to do next. I looked at James and Agatha. "I think I will keep watch Incase anything happens, or we get any visitors, "James said as he made a set of daggers from the blood. He shuffled out the door.

It was only Annabelle and I then. The first time we had been alone since Agatha's bone fortress all the time ago. Before the fermenters, The demons, The Duchess. Ehud and the torture. It felt like a lifetime ago.

Annabelle sat down next to me and handed me a glass of purple water. For a little while, we sat in silence taking slow and thoughtful sips.

"Annabelle, I would apologize I did what I thought I had to do to save you and James. It worked, and we are free. Zadok is alright, and he understood it is what had to be done. I know that what I did was messed up, I only did it because I care about you," I said

I was distracted by Annabelle's beautiful brown eyes. She looked at me and scrunched up her lips to one side and then the other. Mulling over ideas as to not say the wrong thing.

"Catalyst, I appreciate you rescuing me and everyone else. Again. I'm sorry that I was with Zadok, he is not a good man, and now I know this. Ever since I saw you, I have been drawn to; you drive your loyalty to your friends, your never-ending passion for doing what is right against everything else. As much as I could see us being together, I don't know if we can be as much as I want someone to stand by and be with until the end of time. I have always been worried that if I get close to someone, they will leave me, or I will lose you I mean them", said Annabelle. She looked away.

"Everyone is afraid to lose people they care about, look at all the things I did to keep myself from losing you though, I don't think it will be that easy to get rid of me. I think we should at least try,", I said.

I paused before Continuing. Annabelle curled her thin fingers around mine. She tilted her head and pressed her lips against mine. I slid my hand onto the side of her face, and we kissed soft and slow.

I heard a sudden scurrying of dozens of tiny feet, the shifting of dirt and debris. The hair on the back of my neck stood up.

"AAAH WHAT THE HELL IS THAT!" Annabelle screamed. Gigantic dog-sized cockroach filled the room. They slurped the black goo that formerly as dinosaur man. Five. Ten. Twenty. They filled the room. They covered the floors and then the walls and the ceiling. They ate everything. A large black one began to bite my shoe. I placed my hand on his big oily gross body. I attempted to poison him with cobra venom, but the oil he was secreting would not let the venom penetrate his thick hull. The cockroaches began swarming around us and closing in. I reached for a sword; they had used their string teeth to devour it to the hilt.

I tried to stand to my feet; I felt the cockroaches crawling up my legs and pushing down on my torso. They began to eat my suit. Starting with my shoe. I wriggled and tried to break free; the bugs began to bite their razor-sharp teeth into my toes.

Their teeth were sinking into the bones of my smaller toes. They start to be ripped off and bitten clean off.

"AAAAA HOLY FUCK," I screamed as the pain shot up my leg, and my screams echoing through my ears.

SHWUCK all at once, the creatures stopped biting my toes, and his head fell into my lap. I looked up to see Annabelle's chakram. She had thrown it hastily across the room. Her face filled with as much surprise as my own. Annabelle and I stood back to back. Slashing and tearing open roach after roach they kept coming and coming. Our arms grew tired, and we grew weak.

"You guys need a hand?"

James's massive frame pushed through the door. He brushes a pair of Cockroach feet off his shoulder. He plowed through the roaches. Swinging a massive blood sword through the air and cutting the roaches in half. He held both sides of the sword, and it split in two, each with half a cross guard. He fell to the ground from the amount of blood he lost creating his blood weapons. Annabelle patted his head off with a piece of his shirt and tended to him while I killed the last roach while he tried to chew through the blade.

"James, JAMES, wake up dude wake up!" I said as I tried to shake James awake. "we can't stay here man they are going to keep coming. We are going to get back to the Mach infinity, that's where the other is headed with the dead bodies, we'll try to think of ways to fuel the ship on the way.

I grabbed some planks of wood and used one of the Chakram to chop down a pillar. Annabelle grabbed the other blood blade and drove it through the center of the wooden cylinder. We rigged up a wooden gurney type device. Annabelle helped me rock James up and onto it. We pushed him out into the hallway and killed any stray roaches we came across. The hallway was dark, and the only source of light came from a chimney-like shaft stretching up the center of the room from the top of the building to the ground floor. We pushed James into a wooden platform. I looked around for a mechanism to take us to the ground floor. All I saw was a large metal chain. I have it a slow tug, and the platform tilted, and James rolled forward. Annabelle leaped to the opposite side from me and adjusted the parallel chains. We eased the platform down the shaft. It descended into an abyss of darkness.

All sudden, there was a bright blinding light, and I realized it was the first time I had seen natural light on weeks. No wonder Zadok went nuts after not having any light for years. We walked along pushing James. Our weapons poised and ready. Agatha had one of her chakras. The other was around James' wrist. I clenched James' blood sword in my hands and gently ran my fingers over the blades. I worked up a wad of saliva in my mouth and spat cobra venom onto the blade.

In the dirt laid several divots. I looked at Annabelle, and she said, “I'm guessing that's where the cosmic carriage was and they already headed back towards the *Mach infinity* without us,” said Annabelle

She looked at me, and for the first time her eyes were filled with fear. She squeezed my arm and looked to the grey horizon. Once again, we had been let down. I knew there was a chance they would head to the ship without us what would they do? Leave without us? I looked at the horizon were the valley lay. The valley we had fought so hard to get out of. The trials we endured and the Villains we defeated. Through all that at least I could rely on the others. I could not even defeat some stupid roaches. The only reason we made it through is because of James and Annabelle. He is in comatose, and Annabelle is tired and beat. How are we going to possibly walk across the valley and the rivers and the acid lagoon? Let alone find a way off this planet.

I slid my way down to the floor and rested my hand on Annabelle's. She curled her fingers around mine and rested her head on my shoulder. Annabelle lifted the cover of her tattered and torn book and jotted a few sentences inside.

Chapter Eleven

Nighttime fell, we had to start on the day-long trip. We had no food, No water and no shelter from the elements. It was either take a chance at dying in a building with no supplies or die on our feet at least attempting to go somewhere where we might survive. I took off my outer space suit and placed it over James's face and arms to shield him from the razor wind if it were to pick up.

We walked and made small talk, as we tried to stay awake and alert. At least we did for a while; however after several hours of walking we were low on energy. The black dust kicked up and into our faces with e step. E time I lifted my leg to walk, they seemed to get heavier and heavier. WHOSSSSSSSSH. I heard the razor wind picking up in the distance before the wind could reach us Annabelle and I pulled James to the floor, and we tucked our heads and chest under the wooden gurney. Using our suits to cover the sides of our makeshift shelter.

With each gust the wind came closer. SSSSRIP. The wind pulled and tore at the spacesuits. Then the wind stopped, and there was nothing. We began to leave the shelter when thunder CRASHED, and the sky opened, and rain came pouring down. I ran a tongue over my dried and chapped lips. Hair was matter to my sweaty forehead, and my tongue lay limp and dry. I was panting from exhaustion, and I would do anything for a drink. I slid out from the shelter and stood to my feet.

Annabelle tugged at my shirt and shouted something; I could not make out what. I stuck out my tongue and realized what Annabelle said. I felt the drops of acid hit my tongue and started to burn it. I dove under the gurney, not before several drops of the rain rolled down my back. I scooped the black dirt into my mouth until the burning stopped. We sat in silence and crowded around James's large frame; our feet and part of our legs extended beyond the edges of the gurney. A low hissing as the acid tried to burn through our space suits. I smelt the melting plastics and metals and was waiting for it to burn my skin until the rain turned off instantly as if it were in a switch.

"Do you think it's safe to go out? The acid water should have recited by now, don't you think?" Asked Annabelle. I peered out of the second-rate shelter. The black dust and soot had begun to settle, and the sky cleared.

"We better get moving again, or we'll never have a chance to get back to the ship or the others," I said. It took us a while, we finally managed to get James back on top of the gurney. We set out once again into the valley which was once the home of the Duchess of death. The wind picked up once again, and I could swear in the mighty gust I heard a familiar laugh.

Alas, we had to move on. We had to keep going. We walked for miles. Our pace slowed, and our steps grew less and less frequent. Annabelle collapsed from exhaustion. I pulled her into my arms and held her close to my chest. I grabbed our space suits and wrapped the arms around the gurney and the other around my chest. pulling the gurney forward. One step at a time. With each passing moment they seemed to get heavier and heavier. The straps dug deep into my shoulders. The gurney tugged against the ground. It felt as if I were pulling an anchor. I took one more step, and I fell to my knees. I tried to keep moving, carrying Annabelle and scooting forward on my knees. I pulled my dried and cracked lips apart. Running my tongue over the itching and burning cuts. When I collapsed and the last thing, I saw was Annabelle's blond hair and colorful outline pop against the black and white foreground of the planet.

"Are they going to be ok? Why would they come out here, I told them to stay there and that we would be back," said Toni. I barely opened my eyes. I recognized Toni's voice; I wanted to make out who he was talking to. I faintly made out Zadok and Gabriel. I tightly closed my eyes and pretended to be sleeping. When I was little, I use to pretend to sleep whenever my uncle would come in. He would let me stay asleep if I was sleeping if he walked in and I was awake when I didn't suppose to, he would hit me and do test on me. He would always catch me because I would close my eyes to tight. That hunk of garbage taught me a lesson after all. Don't try so hard sometimes; things require less effort. I loosened my eyelids and barely closed them.

"We need to get the ship fully functional. Because we can hover does not mean it could fly. Let us restrain them. Catalyst does not give up easily. I say we restrain them. Fix the ship make the fuel and then leave this planet," Zadok said as he paced the room running a rope through his hands.

Toni stroked his goatee, and he formed his thoughts carefully before he spoke.

"We can't do that! He saved us; they saved us. We would not be here if not for them, and I will never turn my back on them. We need to band together not divide us. We have a better chance of surviving if we all work together. No army has ever succeeded by being divided." Said Toni. Zadok walked over to where I laid and bent down to wrap the rope around my wrist.

"You want us to play nice? Catalyst was the leader, and now I am. You do not think he will try to take it back? Lead things the way he wants to. The best defense is a swift offense." Said Zadok. Gabriel hovered above the ground and flew over to me. He dropped a bead of acid on the onto the rope in Zadok's hand. Gabriel Said "I am not Catalyst's best friend, and he did get my friends is killed. I would take you're approach Zadok. I truly would if Catalyst could beat Ehud and his army of Dinosaur men after weeks of torture. Us tying him up with rope along with his best friends would be the worst and probably last thing we would ever do. Wake him up."

I bolted up in bed and pushed aside the rope that was laying on my chest. I stood to my feet and walked over to Zadok. Stared into his eyes and said, "you don't have to like me, you don't have to follow me, and you have to work with me to get home. If you get anyone hurt, I promise you will pay." I turned and walked to where James and Annabelle we're lying. Agatha and Reuben had been taking care of them while I was asleep.

Toni flipped a switch, and a corner of the room lit up. The light reflected off the blades of a couple handmade swords. Toni walked over and threw one to me and one to Gabriel.

"What brings a group together more than sparing, fight each other, fuel each other train each other. Now while the computer runs a test of the exact formula we need for fuel and a damage report, I say we practice fight no holds bar when we get back to Earth, they will throw everything they can at us. They will show no mercy, so maybe we shouldn't either ", said Toni. When he said the last words, he looked at me for the disappointment on my face. Ssshhs, the sword slid across the floor, and I stopped it with my foot. I reached down and picked up the crudely made blade, wrapping my fingers around clunky hilt.

"Let it begin!" Shouted Toni.

I moved the blade of the sword through the air, feeling the weight and adapting to the bend of the blade. Gabriel lunged, and A loud CLAG rang through the air as our blades collided. I twisted my wrist, and his blade slid off the end of my sword. I kicked his chest, and Gabriel hit the floor.

"Oh, you want to fight like that, watch this" Said Gabriel. He flew up into the air and cocked his sword back ready to strike. I raised my blade to block his sword. I rolled out of the way before our blades connected. I jumped to my feet, and Gabriel shot into the air once more. I grabbed his ankle and slammed him to the floor. His blade hit the floor and shattered — the tip of my sword connected with Gabriel's neck.

"Gabriel, you have lost, good fight not good enough" I said sarcastically. Schuck. I heard his claws extend. It was too late. His claws cut my blade into metal chunks, and they fell to the floor. I swung at Gabriel and my first connected to his face. We rolled around on the floor until we started laughing.

"well, I guess that's the end of sparing since we broke both swords," I said in between laughs. Gabriel had started to laugh before his face turned dark and serious.

"You know you're not half bad at fighting, you weren't half as crappy as I thought you were," said Gabriel. I turned to respond when I heard Annabelle shout from the other room.

"Catalyst! Where are you, what happened?" Said Annabelle. Her knuckles locked tight around her chakram. I heard the chakram cut through the air as it embedded itself behind my head. It barely cleared my ear. She began to hyperventilate, scream, and panic. She flung her arms wildly, and body bounced off the table. I pressed her shoulders against the metal.

"Annabelle, it's me! It's Catalyst. We are back aboard the ship. James is safe. We are all safe. Toni came back, and they rescued us from that desert. Everything will be ok, "I said. She stared into my eyes and studied my face for a moment. She wrapped her arms around my neck and kissed me.

"Hey Zadok, still up for training me with that chakram? It's time to help me become the badass I know I can be," said Annabelle. Zadok walked over and ripped the chakram out of the wall and handed it to her.

"Let's get started, we will train while they finish the fuel," Said Zadok.

He set up lots of targets, cans, empty containers, chunks of metals. Annabelle threw the chakram over and over at the different targets. She missed several times. E round, she would miss fewer and fewer objects. Until finally she had cut almost all of them in half.

Toni and I checked on Agatha and Reuben, who guarded the dinosaur bodies. We attempted to make the fuel. We began to walk out of the door, and the last thing I saw was Annabelle held a Chakram in each hand and practiced her melee skills. Zadok's eyes glowed goldenly and he pulled out a middle-age long sword from his amulet.

We continued through the door's threshold and heard the clanking of metal on metal.

"Toni! Gabriel! Catalyst! We figured it out Reuben found the perfect formula and exactly which ways to use his powers to make the fuel," said Agatha.

Everyone gathered in what was left of the main cockpit. We stood around what was left of the chairs, and we tried to hold on to the wall. We were all excited, and in wonderment as Reuben pulled aside a door to a room I had yet to be in. The smell of death and decay filled the air. The smell incited a flashback to when we were fighting the fermenters. I could picture the fermenters long scrawny fingers wrapping around people's arms and fermenting their bodies. The purple and black rotting flesh filled my mind in vivid details.

"Catalyst? You alright, man. Hello?" Toni asked as he shook me back into reality. I checked on James, and then turned back toward Reuben.

He touched the dead dinosaur men on the forehead and changed their state of matter. They began to melt into black puddles of elements. Zadok cut hole in the floor that connected to the fuel intake. The liquid hydrogen meshed with the liquid oxygen. Zadok's eyes glowed golden once more, and he returned the long sword to the amulet and pulled out a tinderbox. Gabriel grabbed a chunk of the sword from the floor and dragged it across the flint. Creating enough heat to warm the fuel intake. The ship lifted even farther off the ground. The computer lit up and said, "launch sequence activated, where would you like to go Catalyst."

I smiled before answering. I hugged Annabelle in excitement turned to front of the ship, and said. "Computer, take us home."

Chapter twelve

A low hum emitted from the heart of the ship. I smelt the burning fuel made from the dead bodies. My nostrils twitched at the stench. The thrusters began to flood, engaged, and the ship lifted off the ground.

The main computer screen rolled back, and the giant windshield was revealed. A loud thunderous clap erupted, and the rocket boosters propelled us.

Gabriel, Zadok, and Agatha were in awe of our ship.

"Instead of having an autopilot for landing or as an emergency, the ship's main pilot is the computer, and you're a pilot are the backup?" Asked Gabriel.

The ship started the last phase of the launch sequence, and we began the lift-off. The ship took off like a jet and began to start flying faster and faster, shredding through the air. The black soot-covered floor whizzed by faster and faster. With every passing minute we climbed higher and higher into the sky.

The computer flashed once again, and speakers popped and said, "*Mach infinity* approaching edges of the atmosphere."

Annabelle squeezed my hand, and even Zadok nodded and smirked.

MALFUNCTION, MALFUNCTION, MALFUNCTION. The computer screamed and screamed.

The ship began to shake and shutter. We were thrown around the cabin and slammed into the walls. The ship began to corkscrew out of control. The emergency red lights flashed, and speakers blasted. The shrill sounds pierced my eardrums. We inverted, and my feet touched the ceiling. I reached for something to grab; the closest thing was a seatbelt. I grabbed hold and held tight and wrapped the belt around my hand. I pulled myself tight against the wall and caught my breath.

Crates and chairs and an empty gurney slid past. The sound of screeching metal filled the room. We stopped tumbling and flipping. The ship slammed into a mountain, jutting everything loses again. I saw someone slide by and I jerked my wrist to grab them. My hand was caught on the seatbelt, and the ship hit a boulder. I was thrown back into the ceiling. My black burnt wrist snapped, and the pain shot through my arm. The spaceship slid to a stop at the base of the mountain, and everything became quiet.

"Annabelle! James! I screamed. Toni, Agatha! Anyone? I screamed, no one responded.

I laid back against the hard metal ceiling and drifted out of consciousness.

When I woke up, the ship was almost pitch black; I could only make out a few shadows and faint screaming in the distance. I stood to my feet and pulled on the seat belt until it finally gave away, and the buckle snapped. I slipped, so I placed one hand on a wall for support. The wall began to melt, and liquid metal began to roll down my arms like a bead of sweat. I stepped back, and in the dim lighting I could barely make our Reuben and Gabriel.

Gabriel's eyes narrowed, and he whispered in my ear.

"So far it's us, don't worry about Agatha we haven't found her yet either thanks for asking, "Gabriel snarled then paused a second before continuing, and he ran his clawed fingers over the crest of his head.

"Something tells me this was not an accident, Toni and Agatha had everything perfected nothing should have gone wrong and yet three minutes after takeoff we crash for no explained reason I bet if we look at the engine. We will find sabotage."

I looked at Gabriel and then at Reuben. I grabbed my pant leg and tore a big chunk of the suit off and made a makeshift sling out of it. Pulling my now busted deformed wrist to my chest and snuggling it tight.

"Gabriel no I don't think anyone would have or even could have sabotaged the ship, why would they. Everyone wanted off this planet as much as you and I. Why would anyone want to lose the only opportunity we have of getting off this planet?" I said.

Gabriel Bowed up to me, and one of his wings twitched. He ran one of his claws across my chest.

"Between you and I Catalyst, I don't think everyone does. Think about it; there are eight of us altogether you really think eight people from different groups, different back stories different periods all want the same things no, we don't know anything about each other. One of us could be lying. What's easier to confront us and fight seven super-powered people? Or to wait for us to be distracted and happy and using the one thing to get us off this planet before destroying it and some of us with it, said Gabriel."

No matter how much I hated him and how much we fought in the past I couldn't help at least agreeing with some of the stuff Gabriel said. The only people I trust are Annabelle and James. Even Toni, I have my trust issues with after he sided with Zadok. I opened my mouth to Tell Gabriel on the parts I agreed with him about when the floor started to shake and give away. I tried to grab on to something; it was too late, I plummeted into a giant hole in the floor.

I rolled a chunk of metal off my leg and looked for Gabriel and Reuben.

"Gabriel, Reuben, where are you? Can you hear me?" I screamed. Once again, no one answered me, and I truly felt alone. My thought drifted to Gabriel's words about sabotage and people. How well do I really know anyone really? All it would take is to lie to me from the start and then continue lying.

Great as if my trust issues were not bad enough.

I was jolted out of my thoughts once more when I saw a bright orange and red flames filling a hallway up ahead. Even though the fire stood yards away I felt the flames and embers heating my skin from where I stood.

"Catalyst! Catalyst, please help me! She is stuck!" Some screamed from near the fire, I shielded my face with my makeshift sling and approached the flames. I could barely see Agatha trapped behind the wall of flames. The fire racing towards her. Gabriel has been the one screaming. He and Reuben were trying to pry a flame covered girder away from the base of the fire

I tried to wrap my good arm around the girder. The metal burned my skin, and I jerked away. Agatha's face red from screaming. "Please help me I don't want to die," Agatha screamed through her tears. She stomped at the base of the flames to extinguish it.

Gabriel freaked out and blasted black acid back and forth. Gabriel Laid back against the wall, exhausted. Reuben and I slumped to the floor trying to catch our breath.

BOOM. Aloud burst shot through the room, and my eardrums rang. I saw the black acid that covered the floor catching fire and the room was set ablaze. The blast shot is backward and slammed me into a far wall. Reuben laid unconscious on the floor. My eyes clouded with thick black smoke. I felt it deep into my nostrils and cake itself in my lungs. I tried to cover my mouth to block out the smoke. The stench burned my throat, and smoke stung my eyes. I covered my head. I could barely see through the translucent garb. The flames spread faster and faster. It traveled up Gabriel's leg, and his flesh burned. Between the pain and the smoke Gabriel passed out. I still could not reach him. I tried to run across the room; the Flames blocked most of the path. I hoped and prayed that Annabelle, James and the others were alright. I smelt the flames eating away at Gabriel I knew I had to do something I began to walk into the fire before I took a few steps the heat was in bearable.

Agatha awoke and panicked. She screamed and screamed for help.

"Catalyst! You must help him! He's going to die; I've grown to love him! I need him!"

The fire had burned more-of Gabriel. His singeing Hyde burned slower than flesh. I tried to rush the fire once more. I was knocked down to my butt I laid on the floor exhausted bullet sized beads of sweat ran down my forehead.

"No, I won't let you die!" Agatha screamed as she threw her hands into the fire as if she could claw her way to Gabriel. Dirt, sand, and mud began to spurt from Agatha's hands. The sand doused the flames. The fire was extinguished, and the room turned pitch black.

We wrapped Gabriel's feet and ankles as best as we could with what we had on hand, which was not much, mere scraps of cloth from our suits and packed the wounds with handfuls of Agatha's mud.

We rested for a long time until we regained some of our strength, and then we went to investigate the ship's damage further.

Gabriel was dazed awake he had one arm wrapped around my shoulder and the other wrapped around Agatha's. Reuben finally awoke, and he took point. We walked through the near pitch-black room. The only light emitted from Reuben's ring. A dark green glow highlighted his path.

Reuben placed his palm flat against the metal. It liquefied and oozed to the floor.

I felt a cold shiver run down my spine, and I stepped into the next room.

"How far do you guys think we are from the engine room?" Agatha asked.

I had stared at Reuben's ring for a long time before responding.

"Agatha it is dark in here, I don't know where we are or how far away the engine room is, or the others are, I think we should follow Reuben and meet up with the others first," I said

Agatha had turned to complain when we were blinded by the lights. I covered my eyes with my free hand at the same time I scanned the room for whoever or whatever had returned the light.

"Catalyst! What the hell happened, I'm out for a couple of hours, and you find and crazy the ship." Said, James. I slid Gabriel onto Reuben's shoulder and ran over to James. Sliding my hand across James' palm and pulling his arm and body close to mine and squeezing him tight.

"Damn I missed you, man, you have no idea; we went through some crazy stuff, and I am afraid it is beginning," I said.

James took a glance around the room and into the next room that was completely scorched and burned. I looked all of us up and down, examining our wounds.

"Catalyst, I missed you to bro you have no idea, I thought I was dead man, thanks for having my back. Hey, you still kind of suck, though." Said, James

He let out a big hearty laugh and decked my shoulder we walked forward once again. Looking back to make sure we didn't leave anything usable behind.

James and I took the lead, the others followed behind. We walked for what felt like an eternity, each minute passing slower and slower. We checked the hallway after hallways. Aside from the minor scuff or dent everything seemed to be fine. No cut wires, no other fires, no blaring alarms. Sadly, there was also no sign of the others. As much as I hated Zadok I hoped Toni and Annabelle had made their way to him. They would be able to keep each other safe.

"I know you're worried about her; she is strong and a badass I'm sure she is alright. If anything, she is probably taking care of Toni and Zadok,"

I laughed a little bit and smirked before responding.

"I'm sure you're right, James, the thing is, and I don't ever worry about anything. We have been on this crazy-ass planet for months, and I've never worried once. Annabelle I am worried about right now." I said as I ran my fingers through my hair and down the back of my head.

A loud metallic echo emanated from under our feet.

"Hey Reuben, think you can make me a peep hole?" Reuben bens down and dragged his fingers across the floor; two little holes appeared on the floor. I heard the slow trickle as a small amount of liquefied metal seeped to the floor below.

I crouched down to my knees and placed my eye against the newly made hole. Several pieces of complex machinery laid on the floor below. Reuben scooted over to enlarge the hole. He places his hand on the floor; nothing happened. He had been using it a lot the last couple of days. His body is probably worn out.

"It's ok Reuben you've been doing absolutely great I really appreciate everything you've done for us; Toni would be proud," I said before nodding and placing my hand on his shoulder. Reuben cracked a slight smile before returning to Gabriel and Agatha.

"Well, only one thing left to do then," James said as he gently ran his 3D printed arm's ring across his palm for the first time in a long time. He crafted a blood battle axe and raised it above his head bringing the thick blade down into the floor. After several chops a crude opening was cut into the floor. The hole was big enough for me to fit through. James and Reuben Each grabbed onto the battle-ax and they lowered me down to the floor below.

Instantly the smell of crude fuel filled my nostrils.

"James, you Dumbass you're lucky you didn't send sparks into the fuel and blow us all up," I said. Before he got a chance to answer what I saw startled me more than anything. Now I knew why we had crashed and why Annabelle and Toni's perfect plan messed up. Someone had sabotaged it; someone had sabotaged us. Sprawled along the far wall was the eighteen-inch-thick fuel lines that connected the Fuel tank to the engine. All four of them were completely cut through, and the Engine had been completely covered in Fuel.

Chapter thirteen

"Catalyst, Is that you? Can you get this girder off me before I drown in this synthetic fuel? "A voice said from the corner. I peered over and saw Zadok trapped. For once I saw that his cocky and full of himself attitude had subsided, and only his fear remained.

"Zadok, I could leave you here and all those mutinies and the team division. The different views and plans would be gone. Why would I pass that up?"

Zadok's eyes grew large, and he clawed at the amulet at his chest. His hands clenched tightly at the chain.

"Catalyst, you have to save me because that's what you do; you think you're a hero. In fact, you're obsessed with it, with discussing it. You need it because it's all you have. The thing that pushes you is being a hero. You'll save me for the same reason why you didn't want to use those dead bodies," Said Zadok.

I grabbed at the girder and tried to move it enough for Zadok to get free. I thought about what he had said, and I knew he was right. If I didn't save him, then everything, I believed was a lie. If you don't choose to do what you said you believe, then you never really stood for anything.

I kicked my legs frantically as the fuel level rose, and fuel poured from the cut open pipes.

My mind started to spin, and it was as if the room got smaller and smaller.

I pulled at the beam it would not budge. Out of nowhere, big arms wrapped around the beam next to mine, and we budged the beam enough for Zadok to wiggle free.

The fuel level did not stop. I felt it rose higher and higher, and I had to close my mouth tightly as the crude oil began to agitate my nose.

The liquid-filled my nose, and I had struggled to move my legs to propel myself higher. James, Zadok, and I tried to scream they were muffled by the liquefied oxygen and hydrogen, the liquid entered my mouth and burned my throat.

A thunderous sawing sound came below me; I tried to swim out of the way; it was almost impossible to swim in the chemically crude fuel.

THUD. A portion of the floor gave away and dropped to the level below us. The fuel escaped through the hole in the floor. We went from floating and being pushed against the ceiling as we drowned to being dropped and slammed into the floor. My hip crunched and popped after I stood up. Every step I took shot pain down my leg,

"Stop moving, or so help me. I will cut you from scalp to heel, then peel you like an orange," said a voice from the corner.

A thin blade was pushed across my throat. Blood dripped down my neck and pooled between my collar bones. My hand flung back, and my fingers found the neck of the man behind me. I injected a minuscule dose of poison from the hooded pitohui bird. He collapsed and fell to the floor at my feet.

"What are you doing to Toni! Catalyst what the hell he saved my life!" I turned around to see Annabelle run toward me.

"Annabelle! You're ok. I'm sorry I didn't know it was Toni; it's been a crazy couple of days. I must tell you something. The ship didn't malfunction. It was sabotaged. That means we must go back to not trusting anyone me, you and James," I said.

"We have to trust Toni he saved me, and he's been helping us since we got here, not to mention he saved you and James,"

"You're right, Annabelle, your right, be careful, though, alright?"

Annabelle gave me a tight hug. I felt her stress and worry lessen as If she were sharing her grief with me. She ran her fingers through my air, and I felt her heart beating feverishly in her chest. I wrapped my arms around her waist and pulled her even closer. Her arms snaked around my neck, and she held me until her heart slowed, and she relaxed. I looked into her eyes as I gently closed mine and our lips touched. We kissed hard and passionately as her hand travelled through my hair.

"Uh excuse me, can I get you guys a room? Maybe some dinner."

James deep voice from across the room, and he helped Toni to his feet.

We pulled our lips apart and hugged each other one more time. One at a time everyone descended the hole to where we stood. Gabriel had to constantly hover in the air because his feet were to burn to stand on. Since Agatha used her powers her body was weak, and Reuben had put her on James's gurney. Everyone stood around and stared at each other because, for the first time in several days, we were all together. We didn't know what to do next.

I peered over at Annabelle as If to gain reassurance in what I said next. She nodded her head as is she agreed in telling them. Annabelle is a big believer in telling people everything and that not telling people is the same as lying. I ran my hand over my chin before speaking. I gathered my thoughts. The room grew silent except for a sound I had not heard for a long time. The sound on Annabelle scribbling feverishly into her journal. I paced the room and looked deep into the eyes of each of my team members, my friends, my mysteries.

"Guys I know we haven't gotten along the greatest lately, and it is important to celebrate everyone being alive and safe. However, the ship is messed up, and I am sorry to say that someone is responsible for it being messed up. Someone sabotaged the fuel lines. All four of them were cut completely in half. I know that this will cause us to fight and point fingers, it was everyone's right to know," I said

Zadok's eyes turned golden, and his amulet burned bright. From his chest, he pulled a large Sai and pushed the blade to my throat.

"Catalyst what if you're only telling us to divert suspicion away from yourself, it's convenient that Annabelle reappeared moments before this big reveal."

I pushed him to arm's length, and Annabelle tossed me a sword. I grabbed his wrist and bent his arm until the blade touched his chest.

"We are not doing this! Two people know I didn't sabotage this ship. Me and the person who did it. Now back off before I do what I should have done yesterday and sent you to your maker "

Gabriel had flown up to the ceiling and dropped his acid on my sword and my bad hand. I recoiled and took a few steps back. Zadok dived, and we both hit the floor hard. James grabbed his shirt and wrapped it around Gabriel's wings before pulling him to the ground. With a loud gasp I heard the wind get knocked from his lungs.

"Gabriel, Please be ok!" Agatha screamed, she ran over and pushed James away before cradling Gabriel's head in her lap.

Everyone started to push and shove and beat on each other.

"Enough! Everyone settles down. This is not getting us anywhere. Gabriel is messed up, and more of us are going to get hurt now stop Fighting. We need to work together to think of another way to fuel the ship and get home," I said.

"Why so someone can sabotage us again. We're not going to get home. We are going to be stuck here forever. We're no better off than we were in Ehud's prison. At least there we got fed. You claim to be a leader catalyst; we have only been led to demise. Prove me wrong"

I glanced at James, Annabelle, Reuben, and then Toni, and Gabriel collapsed on the floor.

My brain clicked as if all the gears meshed at once, and finally everything made sense, I knew what I had to do.

"Zadok, you're right about everything."

"Excuse me, Mr. Catalyst did you admit fault and that I was correct?"

"Yes, I did, this whole time I thought I was supposed to be some great hero and that team of heroes needs a leader - someone who doesn't fear or kill and that takes all the blame and worry. That's not realistic, and you were right; neither is this perfect hero thing. Everything is not always black and white. Sometimes people try to kill you and if they're trying to kill you sometimes the only thing to do is kill them. Sometimes teams need strong players more then they need a perfect coach,"

I paused before continuing. The entire crew had paused to stare at me in awe; they were all equally surprised and confused.

"The only way we are ever going to get off this planet is if we work together, you and I equal. Everyone will vote on what we should do, like what we were going to do when we got here. So, any ideas on how to move the ship with no fuel."

I heard heavy breathing from across the room and saw Toni start to stir, and he stood to his feet. He rested his hand on Annabelle and James's shoulder when they helped him to his feet.

We should have no problem choosing a different form of power. Liquid fuel is not the only choice right, what about solar power, nuclear power, battery-powered "said Toni

James interrupted him sharply and blurred out.

"What about that radiation power or even the nuclear one. If Zadok can pull items from the past that his family touched, then what if he touched them? *A series of nukes powered the Orion."*

I looked at Zadok, who was stroking his beard and whispering to Reuben. He walked over to where Annabelle, Toni, and I stood. His voice dropped to a whisper.

"What about nuclear-powered submarines? Back in the late 2000s, one of my ancestors worked in the engine room on a nuclear sub. There is no way I can pull something that complicated through time.

We felt defeated and beaten. Toni leaped to his feet and blurted out.

"What about the nuclear power used in projects like *project long-shot or project* AIM Star If Reuben could somehow make a cloud of antiprotons, he could activate fuel pellets. That is if Zadok could pull the pellets through time.

Zadok grabbed his amulet, and it flowed as it had before his eyes glowed golden before shifting to dark orange. He managed to pull the fuel pellets through time and fill a metal barrel with them.

His knees buckled, and he collapsed backwards to the floor. Agatha dabbed his forehead and cheeks with a cloth. Zadok's eyes went from golden to brown as his eyes rolled to the back of his head.

Reuben and I worked on making and controlling antiprotons. Deriving them from other items and elements we tried hundreds of ways and experiments. Nothing worked; after all we're not rocket scientists were normal guys. Annabelle, Toni, and James worked on creating a magnetic nozzle from pieces of our ship and the Cosmic Carriage.

We had tried to get the parts needed for hours and hours. The hours turned to days and then the days turned into weeks. We survived on recycled purple water, and we forced ourselves to eat the only thing we had available — dead cockroach. After several months of that terrible life we finally had a breakthrough. Reuben was able to make antiprotons. Well really, we discovered them as a team because they can occur in cosmic rays detected by the ship. Toni and Zadok got the ship's computer back online. After that, everything was easier.

The spaceship held documents and specifications for the magnetic nozzle and how to obtain the anti-protons. Most importantly, how to turn some of the ship's computers and components to be able to run on nuclear propulsion instead of liquid fuel as well as being able to store and harness them. The team had never been closer. I knew that every one of us secretly still had shards of doubt because of the sabotage and deceit perpetrated by one of us last time we thought we had a sure-fire way off the planet.

Everyone hesitated to attempt a lift-off for fear of blowing ourselves up. The computer ran countless equations and formulas. Toni and Zadok contemplated e outcome. Even the outcome of being sabotaged once more.

"ANALYSIS COMPLETE, NUCLEAR PROPULSION CAPABILITIES ACHIEVED "

Chapter fourteen

I leaned back in a makeshift chair that James and Agatha mad. Annabelle walked over to me and gently ran her fingers lightly down my jaw before gently kissing my lips. She wrapped her arms around my back and hugged me tightly. Annabelle's nose brushed slightly against mine as she leaned down to kiss me more. I had gently pulled her on too my lap and gently ran my fingers up her spine. I felt her sweet, warm lips pressed tightly against mine as we started to kiss.

Once again, our sensual moment was interrupted by the others shortly after it had started.

"IF THE SHIPS READY THEN LET'S GO!" Toni screamed. The ship whirred and buzzed, blared, and flashed. From the crash and converting from liquid fuel to nuclear propulsion.

"Now all that's left is to decide on a destination, earth yes to where what is outside of the presidents reach?" asked James

The engine began to roar, and the ship's computer burst with life, it constantly ran analysis and formulas, options, and outcomes.

She ran her fingers through her hair and closed her journal.

"What If we are years ahead of Earth? I mean, we had to travel light years to get here. The days seem extremely long here; what is one day here is like a week of Earth days. We may have been gone for years. What if everything were striving for and fighting to achieve, no longer exist."

"She is quite right. The chance that this could be a legitimate concern is justly founded. Perhaps we should further consider the outcomes and possibilities before blasting off into a bigger problem than the one we already are not prepared for." Said Zadok

"How about we put it to a vote then, need I remind you that this is what our entire journey has led to. All the trials and torture we have endured all the battles fought. All my friends lost would be in vain. Do you guys so easily forget? That's interesting because I can't seem to stop thinking about them. Every time I try to sleep or relax or even close my eyes, their faces plague my thoughts and my concentration. So, I say we go back to Earth and kill the president and anyone else who's trying to install some global dictatorship. So that the deaths of Sliver and Thermal, Smith and Willard, not to mention Agatha's entire stronghold of people. Most of all Raymond all died and sacrificed Everything so that we could try to make it home. So, I say we do the right thing and honor them and do whatever it takes to get home,"

My speech had moved the others so much they had taken to their feet. Agatha and Annabelle have been moved to tears, and the others I could tell they were trying to look tough.

"I say we do it for Raymond and all those people suffering on Earth," said James

One by one, the crew sat down and buckled up each had their reason for returning to earth the one factor that United us all was still revenge against the NAC President and to bring an end to the United Nations globalist regime and to reinstate freedom to the world.

Zadok's face was stern, and his jaw was tight. I heard his heavy breathing from several feet away. I could almost feel his frustration from several feet away. Several minutes had passed, yet still no one wanted to be the one that activated the first test of the newly donned nuclear-powered engine. Until Reuben entered the bridge and hugged Toni tightly. Toni whispered in His ear for several minutes before giving him one last hug. I gave Annabelle one last kiss before I asked everyone to join me in the cockpit. I heard the click of a draw close as Annabelle locked her journal away for safekeeping.

"Preparing for lift-off count down initiating," The main computer shouted. "10, 9, 8"

The noise of the nuclear engine grew louder and louder

With each second that past. I felt my seat vibrated and shook faster and faster.

"3,2,1 liftoff on test flight one…." The computer was cut off sharply as the ship grinded to a halt against the planet's surface. I slammed back into my seat, and my neck throbbed sharply.

"Computer what caused the malfunction," Gabriel, Toni, and I asked in almost unison.

"It seems something as interrupted the fission process in the nuclear core; repairs must be made before liftoff can be reattempted,"

"James, Toni, Zadok bring your weapons. We don't know what we are going to run into the engine room.

I heard Toni sharpen his sword. The metal is shrieking against the metal floor.

Gabriel, Reuben, Agatha, and Annabelle stayed in the cabin to make sure no one came in.

Our footfall was drowned out by an unfamiliar hissing and spitting sound. Before we entered the engine room, I saw a bright purple light peeking under the door to the engine room.

James clapped his palms together, the loud applaud echoing off the door. He clenched his fist and revealed his blood forged brass knuckles.

James started to laugh over the gnarling and gashing sound uncontrollably.

"James, what the hell are you finding so hilarious," Zadok asked.

"Oh, you don't get it, see bloody knuckles."

He laughed even harder as he knelt next to me so we could wait on Zadok to decide what weapon he wanted to pull through time.

The Familiar golden glare emitted from Zadok's eyes and reflected off the wall as he removed an ancient Tomahawk from the amulet. Before we opened the door, Toni and asked, "Catalyst, what's going on with Gabriel? Is he going to be alright?"

"He honestly hasn't been the same ever since his legs got so burnt he can no longer walk, and thanks to James and me, he can barely fly I think he's getting tired of being on this planet after dozens of years, almost like he can't win. So, let's make sure we get him home," I said

Our conversation ended abruptly when a strange liquid oozed from beneath the door. Zadok dipped the tip of his tomahawk into the ooze, and it immediately started melting forcing Zadok to let go before the ooze reaches his hands.

"James, get the door!" I shouted

James pried the door off as Toni used his bone sword to slice through the hinges one at a time. It was then I heard high pitch click-clacking of hundreds of little feet.

"What the hell is that!" James screamed as he attempted to slam the door against the floor. Zadok fell to the floor and slid along the ground, inching closer to the nuclear engine.

"HELP! HELP! HELP! Zadok's screams were muffled against the metal floor.

I dove into the doorway and grabbed at whatever had hold of Zadok. My hand wrapped around a cylindrical object. I thought it was someone's big arm when I pulled it off him one piece at a time the light glistened off aback. Off a dark shell of a centipede, these insects were the size of small hounds. It began to wind itself tightly around my arm digging one of his dozens of legs into my arm one at a time. I clawed and tugged as the creature dug into my flesh. I tried to poison it, the toxins slipped off the shell, so I did what I had to do. I'd it wanted to feat on my blood I would let it. I stuck my finger into the hole in my arm and injected myself with a trace amount of venom from the brown recluse spider. The centipede's feet retracted, and it immediately curled and fell to the floor.

"Everyone be on guard. We don't know how many of these blood feasting centipedes there are," I said.

"Millipedes actually they have too many legs to be centipedes," Zadok said snarkily.

The millipede I had killed began to seep the same type of ooze as the stuff by the door.

We had managed to enter the engine room when I saw dozens of the millipedes were on top of the Nuclear core feasting on the radiation and emitting the glowing ooze. I heard the swishing of Toni's blade as he hacked through several millipedes. Another millipede has latched onto James' leg, and he punched and squished several more.

Like the cockroaches in Ehud's castle, these pets never stopped coming. I felt myself getting sick, and my vision had blurred.

We had removed most of the millipedes with poison or blades or by squishing the was when Toni had begun to scream. It had gotten harder and harder to hear him. Toni shouted.

"I knew it was too easy; these creatures are like the patriots at the Alamo. Their goal was never to beat us; it was to weaken us break us. Make us go painfully and tear each other apart from within. I don't think they weren't sucking our blood I think they were filling our blood with this radiation laced liquid from their mouths. I opened my mouth to respond the closer we got to the nuclear engine the more our bodies were affected by the radiation. My knees hit the floor, and my vision went dark.

I drifted in and out of consciousness, only able to lift my eyelids for a few seconds at a time. It was long enough that I saw Gabriel for a brief second and heard Agatha crying and screaming.

When I woke up, we had returned to the bridge of the *Mach infinity.*

When I woke up, I heard several people whispering.

"Gabriel why does it have to be you? Maybe we can fix our suits, and we can all go in there and fight them together, we've only noticed how much we care about each other, and I haven't stopped thinking about you or losing you since we found each other in that prison all that time ago. Please don't leave me"

"Agatha you know it has to be me; I am the only one who has an intolerance to radiation! You saw what it did to the others. It nearly killed them. As much as I don't like Catalyst, I still don't want him dead. If killing these and sealing the nuclear engine means a chance you can get home, I have to do it."

They held each other tight, and Gabriel brushed Agatha's hair out of her face, kissing her slow and with passion. Agatha had started to cry and Gabriel wiped her tears away with his thumbs

"Agatha, I love you have to let me go! I know you're one badass woman who can take care of yourself Catalyst and Zadok can help you and fight with you. I know you don't trust them; I think they're your best chance of getting home and getting a good life. Try not to let your stubborn self-get you killed.

Gabriel cried, too, and Agatha's cheeks were catching the rolling teardrops. They hugged one last time, and Gabriel began walking away I heard the quick swoosh as he extracted his claws. His footsteps grew quieter in the distance and Agatha was still crying. I stood to my feet and tugged the suit off Toni and part of James' suit. The helmet clicked into place, and I activated the oxygen rebreather. I didn't know if the suit would protect me from the radiation or not, I'm sure it was better than nothing, and I could not let Gabriel go alone.

Toni and Zadok were still asleep and messed up. There was no way I was going to put Annabelle in harm's way when it could be avoided, and I promised Toni I would take care of Reuben.

Annabelle pulled on my arm and hugged me tightly.

I rubbed her back and ran my fingers through her hair.

"Catalyst I hate to sound like Agatha, you can't go you have no resistance to radiation it could easily kill you or mess you up. However, I'm not saying you shouldn't go. I'm coming with you; someone has to watch your back."

"Annabelle, you're not coming with me, it's too dangerous. End of story."

"You're as stubborn as me; I'm a grown-ass woman. You're not going to tell me what to do."

I did the only thing I could; I dragged my hand across my lips like I always do when I am thinking.

"Alright, your right. I cannot tell you not to come."

I pressed my lips against hers, and she fell to the floor numb.

I lifted my visor and pressed my lips against Annabelle's. I could almost feel her emotions through the kiss. I pulled my lips away and pressed my forehead against hers.

"I love you, Annabelle"

"I love you to catalyst I'm holding you to that promise of coming home to me."

Our hands pulled apart, and I grabbed Toni's bone sword from the homemade sheath and ran after Gabriel.

"Gabriel, I know you're trying to save everyone, I can't let you go down alone. If you're going to die saving us, then so will I. "

"listen, hero, I know you're always trying to do the right thing if we can do this without you needlessly sacrificing yourself. They need you, promise me if I die you will protect Agatha."

I started to speak when He interrupted me,

"promise me!"

"Gabriel, I promise I will do everything I can to get us both back and to get us home if I can't then I will make sure Agatha and the others get home safe and have a place when we restructure the world."

I slide my hand into Gabriel's, and we clasped each other forearms and nodded. We started to walk again, and we're almost to the engine room when Gabriel stopped in his tracks and turned around. Sadness filled his eyes as if he had already decided he was not coming back. He held out his clenched fist until I extended my palm. I closed my fingers tightly around the item.

"Catalyst if I don't make it back at least get this back to Earth and bury it in Tennessee where Willard, Smith, and I grew up. There used to be this big barn where we use to play all kinds of stuff. Army guys and cowboys", he started to stare into the distance, and his voice began to drop off.

"Ironically, our favorite game was always spacemen and planet invaders."

Gabriel turned around to enter then engine room we heard the millipede's feet clicking across the metal floor inside. I uncurled my fingers and revealed three talons attached to a solid black necklace.

"Each of those talons belonged to someone from my crew that we lost, the one on the left is Smiths the center one Willard and the one on the right belonged to my brother Jack Now enough being all sentimental. Let's go kill these bastards and fix the engine before you start liking me or feeling sorry for me or."

We moved aside the broken off doors and laid them on the floor. The room was bright, unlike last time. The second time was worse I saw the black and brown speckles millipedes. The pools of radioactive ooze highlighted the floor. A stench filled my nose that smelled so pungent it made rotting meat and rancid milk seem pleasant in comparison. The millipedes gnawed on the Nuclear engine housing I kneeled to inspect the engine from what the computer had taught me I saw the radiation protective case and case protecting the nuclear core were in-tacked the propellant casing was eaten clean through. A millipede had begun to make its way up my leg and attempted to bite through my suit. I used Toni's sword to cut the millipede in half. Gabriel hovered in the air, his wings flapping fast enough to ease the pain of his legs. He doused several of the pests in black acid. It melted several of them until the rest began to feast on the half-melted husk. Every time I cut one in half, dozens more appeared to take their place.

"Catalyst, if they chew anymore of the housing for the engine, they will hit the radiation core, and it will be moments before everyone on this ship is irradiated."

"In that case, we better start killing them faster than" I screamed.

Gabriel dug his claws into the back of the biggest millipede I had ever seen and dragged his talons clean through cutting the beast into six perfectly cut sections.

"Gabriel now! Lift me"

I coated the bone sword in a thick layer of poison from the golden poison frog. Gabriel wrapped his claws around my shoulders and picked me up into the air. He flew through the room, and I ran the sword through dozens and dozens of millipedes. As the last one was about to Chew through the casing Gabriel let go of me, and my feet crushed the milliped. I felt the ooze squish beneath my feet. The radioactive liquid caked the floor almost entirely. Millipede entrails were strewn about the room. Gabriel and I collapsed onto the floor in a puddle of blood, sweat, and millipede guts exhausted.

"Hey, Gabriel? If we killed them then what's that's noise?"

I heard a faint clicking sound, and the several pops getting louder and louder. A metal roof panel popped, and hundreds of Millipedes and their eggs rained down on us from above. They got to work chewing on my suit as well as the Nuclear engine. I swung the Sword, again and again, attempting to hack through the incredible amount that was now up to knee level. A sea of millipedes ate away at the walls, my suit, at the reactor, and even Gabriel's head crest.

Gabriel grabbed my wrist and pulled me close for a moment we fought back to back

"Catalyst, I have an idea, and it's the only way either one of us is getting out of here with the engine intact. A few more minutes, and they'll expose the radiation. It has to be now, and it has to be me."

I opened my mouth to argue he covered my face with my hands. He started speaking again with a rough and wavering voice.

"We've argued long enough Catalyst. In my entire life, I never contributed anything to society I never left my legacy. Nothing I did would make people remember me; this will."

Gabriel extended his claws and cut one of his talons off. He tossed it over his shoulder, and I caught it in my hand.

The millipedes had chewed almost completely through to the radiation. My arms were too exhausted to swing the sword anymore.

"You have to poison me, Catalyst. It's the only way. If you poison me..."

"Gabriel, I can't poison you; my friend plus Agatha would kill me. There has to be another way."

Gabriel grabbed my hand and placed my palm on his scaly forearm.

"There is no other way. These Millipedes will eat each other if they are wounded, especially if the wounded have radiation in them like my acid and blood. If you poison me, they will eat it and die I'm the only one who can fix the engine without getting radiation poisoning "

BOOM, they chewed through the outer casing, and a small explosion blasted me across the room. Gabriel had flown over to me and grabbed my hand against his crested head.

Dark acid tears ran down his scaly dragon-like face. DO IT NOW!

My vision blurred as my eyes pooled with tears. I placed my finger in Gabriel's eye and filled his body with an immense amount of venom from-the black widow.

Gabriel flew over the Nuclear engine and began to try and repair the fuel line and sources while also repairing the casing of the radiation. He blasted the poisonous acid across the room, covering almost all the millipedes. The ones not covered began to feast on the rapidly melting and decaying ones. The more who ate the acid and poison covered ones the faster they died.

I tried to stand and help defend Gabriel. My legs buckled, and I fell to the ground, exhausted.

"AAAAAAA OH MY FUCKING GOD" The Millipedes starting to eat away at Gabriel as he feverishly worked to prevent the radiation from spreading to the rest of the ship. They took small bites at first, and the then ripped big meaty chunks of scales and flesh.

I attempted to stand my legs shook, and Gabriel's screams still rang in my ears. Gabriel blasted the floor where I stood with acid, and I clawed at the air as I fell. I had to save Gabriel I had to. When I hit the floor, I had to roll away from the Acid.

I knew I had to save Gabriel how would I get back to the Engine room. I ripped off my makeshift suit, and I tried to fasten a rope as best as I could. I tied one end around the hilt of the bone sword, and I heaved it into the hole above my head. I used e ounce of energy to climb back the floor above me. I ran over to Gabriel, and he was mangled and deformed. I screamed, and I cried when Gabriel inhaled, and he sucked all the acid from the floor before it burned through the whole ship. My eyes dropped to Gabriel's twisted body, and his lips were moving barely uttered sound. I placed my ear to his mouth and Gabriel tried to speak in short broken words. His speech interrupted only by the air sucking through his chest.

His voice barely above a whisper "Thank you for the hero's death." I cradled his body in my hands until the life left his eyes, and I placed my forehead to his chest and continued to cry.

When I reached the door, I looked back at Gabriel one last time. All I could make out was the frail, thin bones of his wings. They stuck straight up in the air and allowed me to see his unrecognizable face.

Chapter fifteen

"NUCLEAR PROPULSION CAPABILITIES CORRECTED" The computer's voice echoed through room; I could barely hear it because I was focused on Gabriel's severed finger in my hand. I went back in and placed his cold body onto the cold metal floor and covered his ice-cold corpse with the remainder of my crud suit. For someone I thought I hated for the longest time, someone I could barely talk to without fighting. I was never touched, hurt, or saddened more by a death. I would give anything to argue with him again. I wiped the tears from my face and attached Gabriel's talon to the necklace and slipped it over my head.

I stood to my feet before I exited the room, I took one last look at the cloth draped over his lifeless body. Then I walked through the doorway and sauntered down the hall towards the bridge.

The same thoughts kept fumbling over in my head over. I can't believe he is gone, and I'm the one who poisoned him, how the heck am I supposed to tell the others especially Agatha. If I tell her that I had a hand in his death she'll probably kill me herself. Maybe I shouldn't tell them that I poisoned him. It's not like they're going to autopsy his body.

Are you dumb you pride yourself on being a good guy, Withholding the truth is the same as lying and good guys don't lie? Especially not to their friends. It was settled then I would walk onto the bridge look my crew and friends in the face and tell them exactly what happened and exactly why poisoning my friend and letting him get eaten by radioactive giant millipedes was the only way to save everyone.

I hesitated before I slapped the panel, and the door to the bridge hissed opened.

"Guys, the ship is fixed, they did it we can finally go home!" I heard Toni yell.

I saw him frantically looking around, searching for what I presumed to be his sword. Without saying a word, I slid his sword along the floor.

"Catalyst!" Annabelle screamed as she flew across the room and jumped into my arms, throwing her arms around my necks and kissing my cheeks.

"Catalyst I'm so glad you're ok, thank you for being ok." She turned her head to kiss me; I glanced over at Agatha. This time I was the one who interrupted our intimate moment. Annabelle looked sad and distraught as I lowered her to the ground. The others looked around the room, in their hearts, they knew what I was about to say.

"Guys, Agatha. I truly am sorry Gabriel sacrificed himself so that we could live so that you could live Agatha. He told me to tell you that he loves you and it was the only way ..." POP Agatha slapped her hand across my face and then blasted my chest with sand. It was so strong and so powerful that it knocked me down, and my shoulder cracked as I hit the floor. I slid to the floor and gasped for air. The air was knocked out of me, and I was struggling to get it back. She began to deck me in the chest and face. Part of me wanted to stop her; the other part knew she was justified in her actions and that I was responsible for his death. Blood trickled down my face and shoulder.

"He's not dead! He can't be Gabriel is strong. He is a fighter. He is a survivor!" Tears flooded down Agatha's face as she screamed. Deep down, she knew he was.

I thought she had finally settled down when she raised her hand to my melted black arm and forced a razor-sharp rock through my wrist.

"Aaaa, what the hell are you doing, I was only letting you knock your frustration out on me because I felt you were due that and I owned it to Gabriel. If you do not stop, I will fight back."

Agatha created another sand spike and was twisting it through her fingers" she wound her hand back.

Reuben grabbed her wrist and removed the weapon while James and Toni restrained her. Zadok pulled out a handkerchief from the amulet and handed it to Agatha.

"I didn't know Gabriel that well, he saved our lives, and for that I am grateful, this handkerchief belonged to the great Martha Washington." Zadok turned and sat down on the far side of the room.

"Hurting Catalyst won't bring Gabriel back. None of us were there, so we will never know how hard it was to make that decision I'm sure it was not made lightly. I think he would want his death to bring us together in unity and divide us," James said.

"Well guess what mister loyal I don't care, Gabriel is gone, and it is all Catalyst fault killing him won't bring Gabriel back, it will sure feel good," Agatha said as she rubbed her hands together. She snapped her wrist and sent three sand shards into the air hurtling toward my head.

Swish. Swish. Swish. Toni has swung his bone sword and cut all the sand chunks into pieces.

"Enough! No more I'm sorry for your loss I am going to miss him too I am grateful we have a mission and we could be going home right now to replace it I say we have a funeral for Gabriel first. ," said Toni.

Agatha settles down, for the time being, she sat in the corner of the bridge with Annabelle and Zadok. Her eyes pierced my soul, and she stared at me for hours. James and Toni carried Gabriel's wrapped corpse outside. We travelled a few miles east of where our ship was stationed. I stuck a crud shovel into the ground and began to dig. After what felt like an eternity had passed, we lowered his body into the hole.

“I think instead of a funeral for Gabriel; we should also have a memorial service for everyone we have lost to be standing here right now” Said James.

We all looked at each other and in agreement taking without words.

“I think that is a good idea, James, before we leave this planet, we should honor all the people who are responsible for us being able to go home”

My eyes ventures around the wilderness outside the ship. The black and white landscape still messed with my head. It was still so dark and dreary. The ink-black trees jutted us of the ground sporadically. We picked a spot between several of the trees to bury his body. Next to Gabriel’s burial plot we posted a picture of Raymond and drawings of Willard, Smith, Thermal, and Sliver. We buried little shards of metal for each of the other Twenty of such people that had once lived in Agatha’s bone fort.

I reached down and grabbed a large handful of dirt in my hand. I stepped up to Gabriel’s grave and stared at the lifeless body covered in cloth. For a moment I didn’t speak; I stared into the hole.

“Gabriel and I fought for almost the entire time I knew him. I wish I could take back all those pointless fights if it proves anything it is that we were brothers. Through my entire heroes' journey it is that there are many different types of heroes. The last thing Gabriel did was go into a fight he knew he couldn’t win so that we could live. Gabriel thank you for teaching me, befriending me, and saving me. I uncurled my fingers and dropped the dirt into the grave. James stood up next to speak about Raymond and Gabriel. BOOM. My eyes travelled down to the floor I reached down and picked up the stem of a flower.

"Fuck your catalyst and fuck you all, you have taken everything from me. My home, my friends, and even the love of my life, and I swear to God I will kill Catalyst if it's the last thing I do," Agatha screamed.

She threw a handful of the black spiky flowers where Annabelle, Zadok, Reuben, and Toni we're sitting. They tried to shield their faces, Toni's face was hit with the blast, and he screamed as his face burned and bubbled. James lunged and tried to grab Agatha when she touched the floor and turned the ground into quicksand. I could no longer feel my legs as they sank farther and farther into the cold ground. I flashed back to when we began this journey, and I had sunk into the planets crust, and James had to pull me out. This time James was fighting Agatha. I kicked my legs and tried to swim through the dark grey quicksand all it seemed to do was kick up black soot. I knew Agatha had to be dealt with there is no way o could kill her or even hurt her. We would have to detain her until we arrived at home.

Agatha began to blast more and more sand into the quicksand making it harder and harder to float or trudge. Zadok had pulled a quarter staff from his amulet and began sliding it over the top of the quicksand to me. Agatha shoot sand into James' eyes, and he began to scream and Fell backwards into Gabriel's grave. "No! Stay away from him!" Agatha said. While she was distracted, Zadok swung the staff and wacked Agatha on the side of her head and knocked her out. We tied her up and escorted her to the brig.

Annabelle attempted to patch up and try to reduce the severity of Toni's burns. It took most of us to pull James out of the hole, and after we covered it, we had the memorial service we all needed for closure. The outer door slid shut with a hiss, and we all took our seats on the bridge. Each of us took shifts watching over and talking to Agatha it was clear the time on this planet, the loss of her friends and the feeling of being betrayed by her friends had driven her to madness.

Chapter sixteen

We decided it would be best to go to bed and get some rest before trying to blast off back into space. I heard soft footsteps outside the door, getting closer to where I laid.

"Hey, Catalyst? Do you mind if I come in and talk?" I could tell it was Annabelle's sweet voice.

"Of course, I wouldn't mind talking to you, you know I will always make time to spend and talk to you." Annabelle sauntered across the room, her hips swaying seductively. I could not take my eyes off her the entire time she approached my bed. The bedsprings creaked as she slipped under the sheets and nestled her head onto her chest. I ran my hands down her sides and wrapped my arms around her chest. Pulling her closer and closer.

"Catalyst Ever since we got to this planet, it's one really messed up thing happening after another. I don't want to lose you like Agatha had to lose Gabriel. Besides actually dying, most relationships fail. I have always been afraid to get involved with people because I go crazy over the thought of losing them. I never felt the way I feel about anyone else that I fell about you. What makes us different than all those other couples in all the other times and worlds?" Said Annabelle. I stared into her sparkling eyes that shimmered like the moon over a small pond. I ran my fingers through her long enchanting hair, I inhaled, and my nose was filled with her alluring scent.

"Annabelle we are not perfect, and I would never claim to be. I think the problem with most people is they have this idea of this perfect person and this delusional relationship where everything is supposed to work out, and they will never fight. Perfect people are not real, and anyone you view as perfect is going to fail and never live up to the image you have when you meet them. Then they fight and argue and thing since they do; the relationship is a fail. Everyone fights. That's what makes us human. If you dated someone you never fought with, you would have to be the same person and ideas one issue; you'd be dating yourself. I promise when we fight, I will always try to use it to strengthen our relationship and move past the squabbles to be a great friendship, relationship, partnership. People grow, people change, things change. I want to learn and grow with you. My life has not been the greatest one; most of it was awful and dark, and it sucks tremendously, I have watched countless friends die. Never known my real family and bad things happen to everyone I am close to. Some people's lives suck however when I am with you it is like the dark tone of my life Is lifted, and everything is good. If you are with me there will always be good in my life. Annabelle will you marry me?"

Her jaw dropped, and I saw that she was as surprised as I was. She sat there in awe for a moment, then threw he arms around my neck and hugged me tightly.

"Yes, of course, I will marry you, Catalyst I love you, and I can't see my life without you."

"I love you too!"

It started in Europe. They combined communism and capitalism, democracy, and socialism. They created a centralized European government. Which spread the wealth, they employed the jobless and homeless to build homes they used the newfound wealth and knowledge to irrigate the deserts with seawater, fixed healthcare, criminals were sent to prison at sea until they could be rehabilitated. Threats were either killed or exiled to the Outland. It was so successful continent created a coalition that led to success. They claimed we have the lowest crime, no homeless, no poverty, cheapest energy by using solar power, cleanest cities, and environments."

"Hey, dude Wake up! Zadok and Toni said it time to try and blast off, we are finally going to get off this world," said James.

"James, we got engaged!" Annabelle gave James a tight hug as we walked to the bridge. I checked on Agatha to make sure she was alright and would be safe during lift-off.

"Catalyst, if I ever get out of this cell, I'm going to fucking kill you. I wish we would have killed you when we found you in the cave all that time ago. Everyone I loved would be alive, and you would be dead." Agatha screamed

"I could have easily killed you all; we needed you're help as much as you need ours, I truly am sorry for you losing everything I am no stranger to lose, I can't bring them back no one can. If you need anything let me know," I said. I heard the thus of the door behind me my footsteps echoing through the hallway underfoot. I took my seat next to Annabelle, and we all strapped in and prepared for liftoff. BOOM. The thunder of the Nuclear-powered engine roared through the entire ship. The metallic clicking of the engine firing pierced my eardrum.

The propulsion system kicked in, and the ship began to lift off from the ground. My seat shook violently, and the hull began to hum. I looked out the window and could the black trees and grey sky whiz by faster and faster.

"Here we go this is it, Third times a charm!" Toni shouted. The ship climbed higher and higher into the sky. After almost a year on this planet, I could not wait to get home and especially to mess up the pretty boy presidents face. I tried to stay happy thinking about him was making me mad, and positive moments don't happy too often in my life.

I reached over and slid my hand into Annabelle's hand and squeezed it tightly. I smiled and gave her a quick kiss. Incredibly blueish lighting flashed across the sky followed by a sonic boom of thunder. Razor wind lapped against the stern of the ship. I peered us of the window, and space was within our grasp.

Another sonic boom shook the ship, and we were thrown into complete darkness. First the computer and screens turned off then the lights other systems after that.

Once again, the familiar feeling of the ship eerily scrapping the planet's surface rang in my ears. We slammed to a stop, and I was thrown from my chair slamming my chest and head into the wall and then sliding down. I collapsed into a pool of my blood.

When I awoke the ship was still pitch black, and I could not see my hand in front of my face. I felt my fingers twitching in my right hand as if I had regained full feeling in my melted hand.

"Guys what the hell happened, WHAT THE ACTUAL FUCK. WHY CAN'T WE GET OFF THIS HELL HOLE OF A PLANET NO MATTER WHAT WE TRY!" I screamed. No one answered me at all.

"Annabelle, James, Toni, Zadok, anyone?" I yelled. I ran my hand over my head, where a giant bloody gash should have been my fingers only felt a small healed over scrape.

I pulled one leg out from under me and then another. My legs both in severe pain at the same time they were incredibly numb. I ran my hand up my legs, and they were slightly bloated, and I could not move them at all. It was as if I had Pins and needles to an absolute extreme. There was a low humming in my ears because of how quiet the room was.

"Annabelle, please answer me; I can't lose you again!" I rubbed my thighs to try and return the circulation to them, yet the feeling still would not return.

I fell asleep once again because when I awoke, I saw a thin sliver of light coming from beyond the window. I stretched and wiggles my toes and then my foot. Rotating my ankle, stretching my leg and then bending my knee. I eased my way over to one of the chairs and pushed off it to pull myself to my feet. I placed my weight on my right foot and tested my balance. I walked across the room towards the window and the light. Surly, James, Annabelle, and the other had to have left toward the light and away from darkness.

The first thing I had noticed when I first began to exit the ship was an overpowering sweet smell like that of a strawberry. I opened they *Mach infinity's* bay door and stepped onto a part of the planet I had never been to before. Lush green grass crunches under my feel, and the sky was a bright brilliant blue and purple. Beautiful brown and grey trees peppered this new valley, and where I looked were bright green plants and bushes most different of all was that this part of the planet had an Abundance of not only foliage also animals. The chirping of birds filled the air, and I saw them fly overhead.

I heard scurrying in the bushes behind me, I turned and crouched low to the ground. Poised and ready to attack, I began to think of all the poison I would use to subdue a threat. More rustling ensued and then a low tapping sound as if the pitter-patter of teeny little feet. A soft squeaky voice came from inside a bush beyond the ship's stern.

"I promise I don't mean to scare you, and I won't harm you. I came to offer you, aide."

"Well then a little friend comes on out of the bush and let me meet you, have you seen my friends?" I said.

Out of the bush came three feet long multicolored squirrel, like the Indian giant Squirrel from the earth.

"Hi, I'm Duly I saw your ship crash from the sky, so I ran over make sure you were alright. Your friends did come through hearing about five or six other people Two women and three men. They went to go exploring wanted you to rest and regain your strength. It seems you took a pretty nasty Hit." The strange fellow began to rub a weird sap unto my head, and he handed me a strawberry the size of a softball. I kneeled to where he was standing so I could get a better look at the rather strange character.

"Well, Duly it is nice to meet you my name is Catalyst, and honestly I am usually awful at trusting people, especially people I met, so everything about you says you're a good guy. I never eat food from strangers. I'm starving so thank you." I took a bite of the giant strawberry expecting it to be bitter and nasty like everything else about the planet; it was surprisingly sweet and juicy. The most succulent Food I had ever eaten in my entire life. I slurped the juice that had run down my fingers.

"Hey duly do you have any more of those delicious Strawberries?" He looked at me funny, then a giant grin grew on his face, and he scampered closer to me.

"Of course, there is, fruit is plentiful here. I can take you there if you like. It would be no trouble at all."

"Honestly, I would love that much."

Duly began to sprint across the valley, and I had to run to catch up with him. I glanced back at the ship and furrowed my brows. For a crash that rough the ship had surprisingly little damage.

"Catch up, you slowpoke, last one there is a rotten egg" Said Duly. I scrambled to catch up to him; he was running fast. I stopped to catch my breath and put my hands on my knees. I bent over and began to paint.

"We are here, were here Catalyst was here "Duly said as he jumped around me giddy with excitement. The giant strawberries grew in droves all around this little Alcove where we stood. Giant grapes hung in clusters on the walls and watermelons the size of small boulders covered the base of the walls. Most stunning of all was the crystal-clear water. I stripped off my crusty shirt and the remains of the spacesuit. I pulled off my boxers that were glued to my skin. I ran and dove into lagoon of luxurious water. Drinking as I swam and scrubbed the caked-on blood and sweat and dirt from my skin. It occurred to me I had not had a proper bath or shower in almost a year. The water was crisp and cooled the best temperature for swimming too. I dove underwater felt the coolness completely encase me. The sound of the water soothed my ringing ears. I laid on my back and floated I thought about how nice and perfect it was there.

I looked down at my right hand for a split second I could swear it had returned to its black burnt state. I shook my head and dove under the water again.

"Hey, Duly, where are my friends? Weren't you going to take me to them?"

Duly slid down the trunk of a big beautiful oak tree.

"Oh yeah, I nearly forgot I get distracted so easily, let's go Catalyst. Don't forget your pants. "

I glanced down and almost forgot I was completely naked. I washed my clothes and got dressed.

"Catalyst are you coming? We can't stay here forever; sooner or later, it will pour that beautiful clear water from the sky." Said Duly. He excited scampered across the Forest floor and leaped from tree to tree.

"We aren't far now; do you have a family catalyst? My wife's name is Sara, and I have two kids Mary and Luke"

"No, I'm not married, I did get engaged to a beautiful girl named Annabelle though."

"Duly

SNAP! I heard a twig snap in the distance.

SNAP, SNAP. The footfall grew closer, and the feet were running faster and faster.

"Catalyst up here." Duly lowered a branch, and he struggled to pull me up to a high tree branch. A shadowy form reached the clearing where we had been standing.

"pst Duly drop me, I learned a lesson from a lady once jump them before they jump you."

I felt like a stone and landed on the mysterious figure's shoulder, pushing him to the ground."

"huuuuuuuuu" The wind was knocked out of them, and they began to wrestle me to the ground. We rolled around the forest floor, and I sent my knee into their chest forcing the air from their lungs. "Catalyst, Is that you?"

My jaw dropped, and I jumped back surprised and started. For a moment my mouth opened and closed yet no words would form.

The words came out and hesitant as if my mouth couldn't trust my eyes.

"Raymond how can this be I watched you die. The Duchess of death made you go crazy and attack us; we had to kill you. I'm so sorry."

Raymond turned his head and walked towards me, eerily quiet and slow.

"Yes Catalyst, everyone is dead because of you. You should have listened to me if it was not for you; we would all be safe and sound in the Bone fort."

"Raymond, I'm sorry I really truly am! I wish I could save all of you. I relive that moment e day "

He turned and began to walk away, he stopped in his tracks and spun around and shouted. "you are a curse Catalyst. Cursed to cursed."

I ran after him with all my might. My foot got tangled in a tree root, and I fell to the ground and rolled down a small hill. I laid on my back and stared at the sky. Three birds began to fly together in a perfect circle

"Ray, come back! Duly what's happening!" I screamed repeatedly

"Do not be afraid, Catalyst I am here to dry your tears. "Duly wiped my face and handed me a strawberry. "

"Nooo! This isn't right none of this can be real; The undamaged ship, barely being wounded, e being almost perfect. My life sucks this must not be my life. What's going on, Duly what is the truth because this must be an illusion."

Duly ran around me until he was joined by a smaller lady squirrel and baby squirrels. They clipped my legs, and when the giant three-foot animal was on my chest, he pressed his forehead onto my own and said, "Catalyst, everything is only as real as you deem it to be."

Chapter seventeen

The world had started to fade, the bright blues turned to grey, the beautiful green turned to black, and the foliage and trees shriveled up and disappeared. I felt the giant Strawberry turn to dust in my hand. Blood trickled down my forehead and caught my lips. I smacked my lips and tasted the bitter, warm blood. Creepiest of all was when everything grew quiet, and the silence pierced my ears.

"Duly, this place is fake. What is going on, Raymond is dead. Am I hallucinating am I dreaming, am I dead"?

The rainbow-colored squirrel reappeared before he melted and reformed into a large green serpent. He crawled on all his legs and turned his head completely around, thrusting his tongue in and out of his mouth. "silly Catalyst, you've gotten too close to the truth for your good. Yes, you are hallucinating, everything here is you at first you created what you wish you could have now you will be forced to view only the darkness of your fears, "the strange snakes hissed.

I fell to my knees once more,, and the serpent shape-shifted again into a hunched over man. I leaned back to check on him hesitantly when he revealed his face to be Willard.

"Help me, Catalyst! He is coming for me!"

"No! This is not real you are dead, and I'm sorry I could not save you!"

Willard shot into the sky, and Raymond appeared and slit his wings off before Willard fell back down to the earth dead.

My head started to spin before I was forced to relive the death of All of my friends repeatedly. My hands stung as if I had poisoned hundreds of people. I watched myself grab Ray's hair and push poison into his scalp.

The scene morphed again; we were inside the ship's engine room. I knew what was coming; I could not stop it.

"No please stop this madness I can't relive this anymore tears began streaming down my face as I watched myself poison Gabriel and then watched him die.

"Catalyst, why are you crying? Everything is ok, I promise." I looked up to see Annabelle standing in the doorway holding one of the exploding flower's stems

"Annabelle! I missed you so much. Are you real because of so much of this is fake?"

"Catch me if you can catalyst," Annabelle said as she giggled and ran out the door. I smiled and chased after her until a thought occurred to me that she was probably a part of my delusion. Right before I reached Annabelle, James appeared and pulled out a blood sickle a pulled his arm above his head.

I lunged forward to push James back and stop him from killing Annabelle; I fell right through him. His head snapped back, and he screamed. "You cannot touch what is not real!" My eyes were locked onto the sickle as James sunk it into Annabelle's chest with an echoing thunk. Her blood squirted into the air and doused the walls.

"Noooooo Annabelle, James!"

This is not real; this is not real; this is not real. I began to slam my fist into my head.

For a split second I must have regained consciousness because, for a moment, I saw a mysterious room and my friends, and I strapped to tables.

"Guys wake up. We have to escape; whatever you see it's not real!" I screamed.

The blip of reality bled into delusion again as I slipped back into another hallucination.

How the hell am I supposed to escape this? A prison of the mind and fueled by my fear. For one week in my life I cannot use strength, weapons or my powers to escape. How am I supposed to fight my way out of a prison that only exists in my mind?

My thoughts were interrupted when another man appeared before me. A face I had not seen for countless years over a lifetime ago.

"Uncle John is that you, this state of mind makes me relive the darkest times in my life. Decisions I regret making. Is that why I see you here? I'm supposed to think long and hard about why I should regret killing you; that killing you makes me a bad guy. I don't regret killing you in the least because you deserved it. If I were allowed a do-over in my life, I would gladly kill you again."

"No child I appear before you to remind you that you are a failure. You are no hero you could not even save your friends. Any of them. While you dream up me your friends are trapped. Imprisoned in their minds. You have killed hundreds upon hundreds of people. You are not a hero. If anything you are a Duke of darkness. You will never escape, and you will never save your friends.

I watched as my former self killed my buckle with the cruelest poison and the kick his dead body.

After my uncle I watched as my memory recalled e person, I had ever killed in graphic detail. Besides my memories the hallucination would alter and broadcast a false memory one where my greatest fear would occur. The loss of a friend and my failure to stop them.

I ran and ran, trying to flee from the torture from my subconscious. I stumbled and fell into the ground. For a moment I was in some limbo; Between awaken and unconscious state.

A distant voice called out to anyone that would listen. "Guys it's me guys, I'm not dead and neither or you! if you relax, I can try to merge our consciousness.

"Hey, who said that who is here?" I screamed

I was answered only by silence and darkness. Perhaps if I relaxed my brain heard that man again.

"Catalyst, I can help you come to me!"

I looked up to see Annabelle standing in a bright clearing. I ran to her and wrapped my arms around her tightly. Her slow methodic breathing soothed and comforted me. I had begun to relax and be comforted.

"Catalyst, you have to wake up! Come on buddy wake up. After the crash they came for you, and they imprisoned you mentally and physically. You don't have much time after they get what they want or info; they need they will kill you...."

The mysterious man's voice faded away, and I was left standing there in shock and awe I was distracted, and another delusion formed. My childhood dog ran into the clearing. He was playful and happy until I watched myself kiss and let him and my dog feel dead. The dark tears slid down my cheeks once more. I had never felt so alone, so lost, so afraid as I did at that moment. I sat down, and I thought of all the causes of delusions of grandeur. I thought about how I could wake myself from the horrible hallucinations. What if someone had drugged me and the effect of the drug is to force you to reveal your deepest fears and secrets and weaknesses.

If the used a drug to cause hallucinations, what if I poisoned myself with samadarin poison from the fire salamander. I would have to give myself a severe dose enough to counteract my anti-venom from the opossum. It might give me enough time to experience the effect before the anti-venom kicks in. Or it will kill me if it kills me then I guess I won't be hallucinating anymore. I stood up as I placed the tips of my finger onto my temples. I Focused all my strength and will power into injecting myself with poison. My brain flooded with the fire toxin and my imagination went into overdrive. The world around me began to spin and swirl the trees and animals and sky became only bright colors. Splotches of blues, greens, and purples danced in front of my eyes. My eyes were plagued with visions of random people and items. Killer clowns dancing on top of giant polka dot candles. The images were replaced only when I was blinded by a bright white light, and for second, I thought I was dead. My blackened burnt twitched one after another before seizing up and the joints locked.

I peeked open one eyelid, and my eyes darted around the room. The room was like that of a cargo bay it was a grey rectangular shaped room split off into about a dozen smaller sections. The walls were made of solid tempered glass. Each of my friends was strapped to a table in the center of each cubicle, each in their private hell.

I looked down on my arm, and I discovered why I awoke from the forced hallucinations. An IV had been forced from my arm due to a large amount of poison accumulated at the puncture site. I tried to lift my arm; I could not. It was filled with poison and numb until my blood returned to normal by the amount of poison diminishing and the amount of blood returning to normal. I wouldn't be able to use my right arm.

A loud alarm began to bounce off the walls and drill into my ears. "PRISONER AWAKE, PRISONER AWAKE. ATTEMPTING TO

SUBDUE." A computer voice shrilled. Gas began to emit from a vent at the top of my cell. I fumbled to tear at the straps so I could escape and block the gas from knocking me out.

"Catalyst, our minds are still linked I can guide you; you have to trust me. Use the IV to cut the straps." A familiar voice whispered in my skull.

I was hesitant at first as I was of everyone after I had arrived on this planet. I held my breath shoved my mouth and nose into my shoulder, attempting to keep as much gas out of my lungs as I could. I reached for the IV the tiles of my fingers barely able to knock the Fat needle into my thumb. I rolled my fingers around until the IV rolled into my palm. I stabbed at the leather straps that bonded me to the table. Over and repeatedly at least a dozen times until it was only held together by a thin piece of fabric. I threw my shoulders forward and writhed until the first strap was broken. The leg strap was easy I merely unclipped the latch ripped it off the table and clipped it around my waist. The Gas began to stink my eyes, and I felt it tickle my nostrils.

"Catalyst, you're going to have to break through the glass wall; they seal you inside, which means there is no door. If you hit the same spot enough times the glass should shatter."

I heard at least a dozen footsteps approach in the distance. I ripped off the leather strap and swung one end and slammed the metal latch into the glass wall. I swung the other end in my left hand and hit the same spot on the wall. I swung the strap underhand and slammed it into the glass. BOOM. The tempered glass shattered into a thousand pieces and showered the floor. A few glass shards pushed deep into my skin.

"Catalyst now you have to listen to me closely, you're going to have to fight your way out of the room and down the hall to the cages."

I stepped out of my cell and saw Annabelle, James, Toni, and the others trembling and shaking from their horrific hallucinations.

"You have to leave them! If you don't leave them now, then no one will be able save any of you guys because you'll be dead. Sometimes you have to drop everything in order to catch it better."

I glanced one last time at my fiancé and friends and then headed for the door. I grabbed the metal latch in my hands and attempted to coat it in poison. The footsteps halted, and I heard a low humming noise as if a device was warming up.

"Catalyst Return to your cell, and we will use minimal force. Defy us, and we kill you or more accurately make you wish you were dead," The head guard said.

I heard a dozen guns cocking, and at least that many men stepped into sight all around me. I wrapped my hands tightly around the strap and moved one of my feet back as if getting ready to strike.

"No, I would never go down without a fight, either I'm going to escape, or you're going to have to kill me. I will tell you one thing after I kill you guys, I am going to take one of those cool guns. Then I'm going to kill the rest of your friends on this ship." I said.

The head guard man laughed, and then his glare hardened, and his dark brow furrowed. "your dad should have taught you not to threaten people who have their guns on you. "

The men behind me had their guns build into a glove and arm sleeve on their right arms. At first, I was confused then they fired, and it all made sense. Their guns shot thermal energy after siphoning chemical energy from their bodies with the arm sleeves. DOOM. DOOM. The men behind me blasted off several shots.

I tried to dive down and dodge the shots one of them grazed my shoulder and blasted deep into my shoulder blade.

"Aaaaaah what the fuck!" I screamed. I grabbed my shoulder and ran my fingers across the burned and bloody skin. I unlatched the leather strap from around my waist and swung the belt underhanded. WHACK. The metal contacted one guard and the other. I jumped and kicked one guard in the chest while the strap wrapped around another's throat. It pulled tightly, and his neck snapped.

Boom. Boom. boom, another group of guards had begun to fire metal and glass slivers from a large barreled gun. I had caught the strap around one of the guard's legs and pulled him into the path of the glass killing him. I slid across the floor, and my foot contacted the head guards' knee. He fell to the floor and fired a couple shots at my chest. I used one of his friends as a shield and dropped the dead body on top of him.

My eyes burned with rage, and I wrapped my hands tight around one man's neck and the others leg and injected them with box jellyfish toxin – Instantly killing them. I jumped off the dead bodies and leaped into a pile of guards I spit stink ray venom into their eyes. I grabbed one of the thermal guns and returned the guard's fire.

"Catalyst you have to hurry, this is only one squad of men if you do not escape soon many more will follow." I was annoyed. I was sure he was right it was now or never. I tucked the gun into my waistband and slid to the floor. It took almost e drop of energy I had I filled the room with a strand of Anthrax coating all their lungs and instantly killing them.

I fell to my knees in exhaustion and grabbed another thermal gun. My knuckles white against the handles I wipe sweat from my forehead.

"Hello! The voice inside my head, where am I supposed to go now!" I was answered only by silence. I thought I created the man inside my head to free myself for self-preservation.

"You need to slip into the hollow shaft between rooms and make your way to what they call the zoo; it is where they hold the more … beast-like prisoners such as myself." I blasted a hole into the far wall and slid myself between the beams.

I shuffled my feet sideways towards the next room.

"Catalyst the next group of guards is closing in, you have to drop into the Zoo. Now jump!"

I reached into the collar of my shirt and held the necklace of talons tightly in my hands. My thumb ran down the center talon; Gabriel's talon and I took a leap of faith. My feet slammed into the floor with a loud metallic clank. The room was an exact copy of the prison that held me the only difference was the cages were larger much larger. Each cell held a beast inside and the first one I investigated held one of Ehud's dinosaur men.

Chapter eighteen

"Pst Catalyst over here, I'm in the cage on the back wall, get me out of here, and I will explain everything." This time the voice did not come from inside my head. It came from across the room, and I knew who the voice belonged to before I even saw their face. I walked past the various cages each with a unique animal, plant, or beast inside. Several of the cages held beings I was familiar with including a few fermenters, a dinosaur man, several giant cockroaches, one giant millipede, and a roomful of the exploding flowers, many of the cages held creatures or plants I had never seen before. When I reached the back wall, my jaw dropped at what I saw.

"Willard is that you? How can that be I thought you were dead?" After I said it I immediately thought about how similar the circumstance was to the countless ones I had when I was hallucinating.

"Catalyst, I can see the look of disbelief on your face. I can assure you I am real. After all the tests and torture, I am still almost completely there. The only thing I am missing is my wings. Of course, I lost those before they took me didn't I"

He rubbed the jagged nubs on his back as he turned away from the glass and sat down on a small bench in the corner. He started at the dragon-like a reflection in the mirror.

"I noticed Gabriel was not with you when they brought you in, So I'll assume he is dead then. I truly have lost everything." I began to rub the jagged bones on his back again.

"Willard I truly am sorry to have to tell you, he is dead. He died saving all of us so that we could have another chance at better lives. I am forever grateful for His sacrifice I only regret not being closer to him when he was alive. step back please."

I paused long enough to unlatch the leather strap belt from my waist and swung it into the tempered glass wall repeatedly until it shattered.

"Willard If what you said Is true, we have to go now; if not their will not be enough time to save the others before we escape."

He looked at me as if I were a fool spewing the most ludicrous conspiracy theories.

"Save the others? I am sorry Sir. There is no way we can save them. We must go, and we must go now. You have no idea what you're up against. We're going to have to leave the others behind."

"Are you crazy Willard no way in hell am I leave all of my best friends behind. If. Man doesn't have his friends, then he doesn't have anything. You can either come with me and save them or you can stay here and be at the mercy of whoever they are.

The look on his face was a reluctant agreement. He stepped out of the cage with the glass crunching under his feet. I tossed him one of the thermal pistols, and we slid back into walls. As we walked, we attempted to make small talk or catch up; it was as if he could only remember certain things. Willard was different-different. Then again so was I when we thought Willard died; we hadn't even got imprisoned or fought Ehud or met Zadok or lost Gabriel. We walked in silence for a while until we came upon a bright light emitting from a vent.

"Hey, Willard, how could you put yourself inside my head and how come you couldn't melt your way out of that cell?"

he stopped in his tracks, and I ran into him, which forced me to halt.

"These people are Outlaws they find special people, creatures or plants and they capture and extort them. They use whatever they can, sell whatever they want and bend people to their will or the will of the people who hire them. Someone hired them to weaponize the people and weapons of this planet. When they captured me, they strapped me to a table like they did to you. Only they didn't need my acid powers because they had already gotten those from Smith. So, they experimented on me. They slipped this guy into my subconscious. This guy could use telepathy due to consuming a high amount of some mountain plants. Only they killed him so that his consciousness was trapped in my head. They injected me with this drug that would block me from being able to produce the acid than the dumped me in that cell until they could use me again. Or until they wanted to show me off in their freak collections."

"I'm sorry man I had no idea I promise I will do whatever I can to kill these bastards and get you your powers back. Now, what is the plan for rescuing the others?"

Willard turned to me with a look of disbelief and sadness filled his eyes. His next words he spoke hesitantly, and his dragon lips moved slow. He dragged a talon against the metal wall creating a low shrieking sound.

"Before we go rescue them Catalyst, there is something that you have to see. After we steal it, you might not want to rescue them anymore because I promise you it will change your whole viewpoint and strategy because it will destroy you and change who your friends are."

I peered into the great to see several men in chairs watching a giant computer screen other guarded the door.

"What I need to show you will be on that screen, we need to get into that room undetected and as quietly as possible," Willard whispered.

I dug my fingers into my blood shoulder and attempted to pull out the glass shards. They severely cut up my fingers and would not dislodge. Willard's thick skin hand pulled out a shard of the glass and covered my mouth with the other hand. He cut a length of plastic tubing with the glass, and I knew what he had in mind. I Pried our several nails that were holding down wire clamps. I coated them in my poisonous blood and put them one at a time into the length of tubing. SWUSH SWUSH SWUSH. One after another the poison tip nails would embed into one of the outlaw's necks causing them to go into cardiac arrest and death.

"Willard surly the traitor must be Zadok he has been usurping me and undermining me and trying to be in charge since we met"

Willard looked sad as if he wishes he could say it was so.

"Catalyst, I am afraid I can't tell you that because Zadok might be a dick apparently he is a loyal friendly dick. I clipped one end of the leather strap to the vent and wrapped the other around my palm, and lowered myself down. I let in dangle in the air in case we had to make a quick getaway. I made my way to the chairs and sat down. I drew my gun and aimed it at the door I was ready to shoot anyone who entered.

Willard started mashing the keyboard and flying through file after file until he clicked on a list of emails marked, Cardinal commands. The list contained entries from almost a years' worth of files. The first date on the list was the date we had left Earth. My stomach began to feel uneasy as if it had already begun to piece together the mystery before my brain. E date was the day before everything bad happened. The date we entered Agatha's camp before the fermenter fight. The date Ehud captures us. E day before each ship crash. My hand shook as I reached for the mouse to click on the first link.

The screen took a moment to load, and then my heart sank, and I felt dead inside. Worse than I had ever felt, even worse than when I got my arm melted off. The first file was a journal entry, Annabelle's journal entry. At first, I thought maybe they had stolen it and uploaded it after they had captured us, it listed specific instructions about all of us. She must have had one of those pens that can transmit whatever it writes. It told the men where we were, who was on guard what our plan was. File after file, I read about how either she had sabotaged us or how she set it up by telling these mercenaries exactly where to be so that they could be there ahead of us. To release the Duchess of Death, cockroaches, Millipedes. E creature e catastrophe ever death was because of Annabelle. I puked, and I puked, and I puked. After I had read through e file several times, I wanted to punch Annabelle in her pretty face and asked her why in the hell she did these Heinous acts. What her motivations were and what the hell she would be able to gain from all of this. I grabbed the thermal gun in my waistband, and I pressed it up against the computer screen, and I fired again and again until the computer was nothing a pile of melted metal.

"Well Willard lets go, I cannot let everyone else suffer from the actions of Annabelle we have to rescue them and get out of this place and take care of Annabelle."

I used all my remaining strength to climb up the leather strap and back into metal electrical ducts. We made our way back to where the cells and cages were. More guards had arrived and found the previous guards I had killed. I didn't care about being stealthy anymore I was exhausted physically and mentally, and I felt broken. I grabbed the thermal gun and shot several outlaws in the face before anyone else could react. Action is faster than reaction. I spit blood into their faces, and Willard stabbed several of the guards with the shards of glass. As it seemed we were invincible Willard took a shot through the leg. A limited amount of blood trickled from the would because the thermal energy is so hot. We sealed off the door, and I poisoned the rest of the guards with sting ray toxin. Willard was attempting to remove our friend's IV when I approached Annabelle's Table. Her IV was empty, and no fluid was seeping into her body. Her eyes opened, and she leaped to her knees I clenched my jaws as she hugged me tightly and I ran a hand around her back. A few tears slipped out of my eye and rolled down my cheek.

Out of the corner of my eye, I saw James's massive frame bolt up and wince in pain.

"James, I missed you so much, buddy!" I yelled as I ran across the room, and bro hugged James tight. The whole time I was hugging James and giving Toni, Zadok, and everyone else handshakes, I could not take my eyes off Annabelle. Except for the first time I wasn't entranced by her beauty or wit, I was watching her because I knew what she was, and I was afraid she would hurt my friends if I took my eyes off her.

Everyone else's eyes were glued to Willard as if he were a dead man walking. The group hugged and him and got reacquainted.

"Hey, Willard, I don't mean to disrupt this tender moment where are we what is this facility and who are we up against," Said Zadok.

Willard and I exchanged glances and peeked at Annabelle before he responded.

"We are on a ship that belongs to a group of government-hired mercenaries. They are outlaws. They don't follow the rules or laws. They will use any means necessary. They are known as the Cardinals. They are criminals of the highest caliber. Catalyst and I took care of all the men in this sector of the ship; more are bound to follow. We need a plan, and we need one now," said Willard.

Reuben and James guarded the door Agatha we left restrained, and Toni, Zadok, Willard, and I attempted to plan of action and escape, from the ship and the planet. Annabelle had been checking on Agatha; she returned to where the rest of us were talking.

"Are you ok Catalyst, what's wrong? Ever since we woke up you have barely touched or talked to me?" She reaches over to place her hand on my face. I grabbed her wrist and pushed it away.

"What's wrong! What do you mean, what's wrong this whole time you've been lying, faking trying to get us killed? You betrayed us, and you betrayed me!" I screamed in her face. Annabelle looked as if I was tearing her heart out of her chest; she began to cry. When she spoke, I could barely understand her through the flood of tears that poured down her face.

"Catalyst how could say such horrendous things about me; I could never hurt you. I love you." Annabelle tried to hug me,I turned around, and a tear slipped from my eye, and I looked over at my friends who spectated us confused. I was the one who was crying now.

"Annabelle you can stop lying your only making things worse; Willard and I saw everything. The file the directions. How could you betray us, use us, and how could you work with them?" I said. All the other had gathered close and looked as if they were holding their tongues and forcing themselves to be quiet while Annabelle and I argued and screamed.

"Catalyst I had to the president has my family in prison. He has my mother and brothers at gunpoint, and he said if I did not lead the mercenaries in keeping you here on this planet then he would kill them. The reason they captured you is to weaponize your powers. I would have to use this special pen that when I write it sends e word to this ship and the presidents." I hesitated before I spoke because I still loved her and because I knew how much she cares about her mother. If I know one thing it's that we do whatever it takes to save the ones we love.

"Annabelle, I'm sorry while I understand why you did the things you did; I cannot forgive how many people you let die without telling us. We could have helped you. We could have fought these mercenaries together and then got back to Earth and rescued them. You pretended to be our friend you love and use me. You've broken my heart and me…"

Annabelle interrupted me and looked around the room at everyone who thought they were her friends. She looked at everyone who had cared and protected her for so long.

"I wish I could undo what I did. I can't I wish we could have saved those people, we couldn't know what was going to happen. You said that Catalyst. You almost killed Zadok to save me, and I promise I would have done the same. Don't think for once second that what we felt together was fake. I never meant to hurt you, and I truly do love you."

Before I could respond, James screamed from the door. "Guys they are coming, get ready I think they are trying to bore through the door." Toni's sword and Zadok's amulet must with the bad guys or hidden because they didn't have them. I through Toni my thermal gun, and Willard gave his to Zadok. The sound of the door vibrating, and jarring grew louder and louder. The room shook, and sparks flew into our faces. Shuck. Willard extended his claws and posed my hands and was ready to poison. James creates his favorite blood sickles. A small hole formed in the center of the door that we watched it get larger and larger.

"one thing when they break through the door, I say we throw them the traitor." Said Zadok.

Chapter nineteen

"No, Zadok, we don't turn on our own; she is still one of us," I shouted. The hole in the door grew larger and larger while Zadok was squaring up Annabelle and me.

"Catalyst, you only say those things because it's your fiancé for crying out loud. You know if it were Reuben or Toni or especially me you would not hesitate to turn on us for betraying you and destroying your trust, "Said Zadok. BOOM BOOM. The outlaws began to fire shots from their thermal guns through the expanding hole in the door.

"Now is not the time we can argue and vote on it later. Right now, I say let's kill some damn outlaws." Said Toni. The door began to melt away; smoke and an awful smell filled the room. Screaming and footsteps echo down the hall." No, we have to vote now, this witch PLAYED US AND TRIED TO KEEP US HERE UNTIL WE DIED OR THE COULD HARVEST OUR POWERS!" Zadok screamed while his face turned dark read, and his veins bulged from his face and neck. I saw it from both ways I understood Zadok's frustration because it was equal to my own. I felt betrayed more than anyone else. She pretended to love me she laid next to me and cuddled me to sleep e night. I killed people for her. I checked my fist and gritted my face my eyes burned into Annabelle's skull.We flipped over our tables, and all took cover in a different cell.

"A Great colonel once said, don't shoot until you see the whites of their eyes!" Said Toni.

BOOM BOOM the Cardinals broke through the first cell and completely melted it after several minutes. I stretched the leather strap across the walkway from cell to cell. The outlaws emerged from behind the twisted metal wall. The head guard raised a red sword cut the strap in too. I ducked behind the table and cocked my gun and pointed it at the doorway. A shadow reflected off the roof, and I stood up ready to poison whoever came through the door. I heard dozens of shots and the clanking of metal on metal. Then came the sick sound of a sharp blade through flesh and meat.

One of the mercenaries crept into the cell I was standing, and his sword was dripping blood. I kicked his legs out from under him and crushed his knee under my food. He swung his sword at me, and I blocked it with the gun. The blade bit deep into the metal, and the gun began to heat up in my hand I threw it at the man, and it exploded. Blasting me backward across the room. I was dazed for a few moments, and my ears rang. I wiped the mad blood from face and picked his sword up from the floor.

The ringing in my ears began to fade. The screams of people filled the void.

"Catalyst helps me, please help me!" Annabelle screamed. I ran out of the cell and toward the sound of her voice. The room filled with the smoke of the thermal guns. My head pounded, and my eyes stung. I searched for Annabelle but all I found was dizziness. I stumbled and caught myself when I began to stand, I saw Annabelle beautiful face.

"Annabelle, what's going on," I mumbled. My eyelids grew heavy, and I was had trouble lifting them. I felt Annabelle's thin fingers slid down my cheek.

"I'm sorry Catalyst, this is the only way," whispered Annabelle. I fell into an unconscious state, and when I woke up, I found myself once again restrained and imprisoned.

"We should have handed her over or killed her when we had the chance. E time we are close to winning, she is going to do something that keeps us from escaping. Look around Catalyst. Your girlfriend knows all our weaknesses all our faults and strengths. Guess what if we escape and fight, we will get imprisoned and escape and fight again over and over until we die. I was right all that time ago in Ehud's prison. There will always be another cell Catalyst," Said Zadok.

"Zadok, you were wrong. We almost got off the if it were not for Annabelle's betrayal we would have. I was the one who was wrong about lots of things. Things do change, People change, and life is not some heroes journey. There is no woven path -no easy way. In real life the journey is dark and shitty. Lots of people die and when you think everything will be alright it gets worse than ever before. The only way out is never to give up and always see the light at the end of the tunnel.

Trick your brain because sometimes you see light that is not there imagining the light exist will push you. Now I don't ever want to hear you tell me to give up again we got out of that, and we will get out of this. Annabelle will see that we can help her; she is doing what I would do if I was her and she was her mother. Anyway, you get what I am trying to say." I was waiting for Zadok to respond to my rant all I heard was slow broken breathing.

"Zadok, Zadok, wake up!" I screamed but he remained unresponsive. My eyes darted around the room, and I felt my heart beat faster and faster. My breath became quick and heavy, the angrier I got. My friends were no longer bound to tables. They were beaten and bloody; they had deep slashes in their arms and chest. I saw where James had attempted to coagulate the blood; I guess he could not get to all of them. Reuben's leg was still oozing blood above the knee. Toni's fake leg had been completely detached and was nowhere to be seen.

"Ugh what the fuck have you done to my friends? I will kill you all!" I screamed and pulled away from the post I was chained to, my hands were bound at the wrist and encased in a metal gauntlet. I tugged and pulled at the metal chain until the gauntlet cut deep into my forearms.I put one of my feet onto the post and continued to pull on the chain until blood ran down my arms and onto the floor. I had to stop, or I would kill myself. I put my back against the post and slid down to the floor. My arms were uncomfortably pinned above my head; the blood continued to trickle down my elbows.

"James. pst James wake up, Toni, Reuben, Willard wake up!" I screamed until James began to lift his head and bobbed it back and forth while regaining his senses.

"James you have to detach your arm and free us. I tried. I can't without ripping off my arm."

James tugged at his 3D printed arm, pulling harder and harder until finally I heard loud cracking noise and his arm ripped free, his hand snapped off in the gauntlet. He used his now spike-shaped arm to puncture a hole in his shoulder. Coating the jagged arm in hardened blood, which he used to hack at the chain until It broke free.

"Catalyst, I missed you, man, and I wanted to say thank you for all the years you had my back. I love you, man, and if we can't get out of here, we had a great run. "said James. He began to hack and slice through the chain as fast as he could. Bringing his arm up higher with each swing.

"James Thank you for your undying loyalty. I will not quit, what is with everyone trying to quit, I never have, and I never will. "

CLANG. The chain was severed through completely, and I stood to my feet. DOWOO DOWOO.A loud alarm had begun to blast through the building until The Cardinals rushed in. James tossed me at the guard, and I raised my bloodied hands, ready to strike and poison. My hand contacted the man's neck, and I pumped cobra venom into his neck. Only the venom would not penetrate his skin it simply rolled off as it had with the Cockroaches and millipedes. They had made a synthetic light armor like the hides of those bugs. I felt hands tighten around my neck and my throat start to close. I clawed at the man's massive hands to no avail. He dropped me to the ground and began to laugh hysterically. They threw me to the ground and re chained me to the post only this time they encased my torso completely in metal.

"Fuck off you dumb bastards you can't break me; you will never win," I screamed.

"Hahaha maybe not; I mean, we are probably going to win. Hey even if we don't it will be really fun to try," said one of the Cardinals. Thunder rumbled above our heads, and the roof shook.

He raises his hands, and from his gloves hand, he extends claws like that of Willard. He stabbed the tip of one of his fingers deep into my jaw. I heard it start to sizzle and feel it burn as he drew an x into my flesh.

"AAAAAAA You son of a bitch, "I hissed through gritted teeth.

"haha is this not interesting to you? We were able to make synthetic acid and claws like that of ... what were your friend's name, Gabriel?

"How dare you disrespect him and desecrate his grave. I will make you a promise that I once made him. When I get free, I will kill you with the cruelest poison imaginable." I screamed in his face, he laughed even harder as he dug his entire hand into my face one finger at a time and slot dragged them across my face. The entire right side of my face burned and itched and felt as if it was cooking inside and out. Five deep flesh seared black trenches down to the bone. The deepest of which pierced my eye which oozed and bled onto the floor. My screams finally jutted the others awake my body passed out from shock long before I was able to talk to them.

"Hey bitch, wake up." Said a familiar voice as I was slapped awake. When I woke up, I was alone in a dark room. The two men who were with me had been in the cell block when we attempted to break out. One was a dark Indian man and the other a white man with a long beard. Both were dressed in black and red suits and armor.

"I am Harsh," Said the Indian man as he pulled on one of the claw gauntlets.

"Where my ancestors came from in India, it was a common name. It translates to Happy. Sadly, for you it is my job to make sure you are anything"

The other man stroked his beard and sharpened a red blade as he smiled and laughed hysterically. "My name is David, and like Harsh we will break you. See, most of your friends were easy to break they had already given up long ago. We already figured out ways to use the powers of your dead friends, and you will be helpless to save your remaining friends. Once we figure out their powers, we will kill them in front of you. I opened my mouth to speak the only sound that I uttered was a muffled grunt. My mouth was gagged and muzzled, my hand's mound in metal, and my knees locked to the floor.

David took the top of his blade and heated it in heat from his thermal gun.

Harsh stepped forward and dragged the claw down my back. "you seem to have a great many scars. You are no stranger to pain; that is why I know the only way to break you is to tell you the truth about your girlfriend."

He grabbed a pen from his pocket and tossed it to David. David scribbled random words onto a pad of paper on the desk. A gigantic screen blinked to life on the wall behind the men. He threw the pen at my feet. This pen was not the betrayal, and we did not make your ship crash. The pen was not what was special Annabelle herself. The door burst open, and Annabelle herself walked in. She undid the gag and muzzle and kissed my cheek.

"Catalyst, it's time to discuss the future and the past. These mercenaries are not government hired. Well they are. I paid them more, and now they work for me. After we unitized the powers we really will go back to Earth and take over the government and kill the president. Not to sound like a movie villain Catalyst it doesn't have to be this way you can join me, and we can go back to Earth and take it over...."

Before she got any further, I stared at her in disbelief. Shocked at who Annabelle had become or perhaps who she always had been.

"Annabelle you know I can't do that. My loyalty is to my friends, and it was to you. If you plan on taking over the world, then I can't be with you. We were supposed to be heroes. Save the world does not take it over. We were supposed to get married and help them establish a new government, Not become the new government."

Annabelle put her finger to my lips and gave me one last slow kiss. "Catalyst, we would be unstoppable I have powers. When I told you writing was my superpower, I wasn't lying. What I write comes true. I can't make things happen; I can greatly influence them. Didn't you wonder why we landed on that exact part of the planet? Why we met Agatha, Gabriel, and Zadok, and they joined us almost no problem. Things happened because I needed them to happen. Now say the word and I will have them unlock you and you can stand by my side as we write the future and create a new Earth. Or you can stay here and perish with our friends I am sorry, this is the only way.

Tears poured down and I shook my head. "Annabelle you know I can't do that, and I never will I choose them."

Annabelle turned and ran her fingers through the scar in my face. "Then so be it.so we are in understanding I have made it so you will never get off this planet no matter what. Your fate is written and sealed. I might as well give you the last bit of truth and that is the government doesn't have my mother. She was loyal to the president, so I killed her long ago. You can have him now Harsh "

She gave me one last kiss on the cheek and closed the door. Harsh pressed the heated blade into my back and I heard my skin hiss. After hours of meaningless torture, they grew bored and left me alone. I laid in a pool of my blood and vomit. So that was it. This is truly where I would spend the rest of my short days. I was finally out of time hope and reason to live. The light at the end of my tunnel had grown dark.

Chapter twenty

I sat in my cell for weeks not talking, not thinking not feeling anything. Until I started thinking about all the events that led me to this moment in my life. I thought about how James and Zadok has been right and how wrong I had been. If I would have stopped fighting in Ehud's prison at least I would still have Annabelle to love and yearn for. Now I know the truth and I truly must push me forward. Nothing to gain by leaving nothing more I can lose by staying. I had lost everything until I sat alone beaten, scarred and deformed. It occurred to me that There was a way I could win, and it would solve all the problems. It would keep the president and the world and especially Annabelle from getting my power. I glanced up at David and Harsh who stared deep into my soul with their weapons drawn to insure I would not escape. Yet there was one last way to win one last way to ensure that the Cardinals could not weaponize my power. In their hands my poison could kill entire armies with a single blast and that was one thing I still knew I could control. If I poisoned myself, it brought a disease upon myself one strong enough or a toxin and then

I wouldn't even need to worry about my anti venom kicking in. I waited for the guards to glance away before working around a wad of saliva and toxin. I rubbed my arms against the metal gauntlet until my arm wound busted open and blood began to seep out. I swished the toxin around my mouth one last time and began to drip ooze into my open wound. Thunder cracked above our heads once again and I continued to drip toxic spit into my arm. A loud gust of wind rushed through the wind. Except it wasn't the familiar type of razor wind. A sudden cool wisp of air.

I continued to push more and more of my toxins into my blood. Suddenly, the blood and toxin would not mix. The spit would hit my arm and slide off which was followed by an itching and irritation in my arm.

"Hey what the hell is going on I knew we should have put that muzzle back on.?" David said as he walked over to exam me. DOOM DOOM DOOM. David and harsh slumped to the floor unconscious. I glanced around the room to see little chunks of everything.

"It's ok I know the way out and the way to the weapons let's go Catalyst… "

I cut her off mid-sentence surprised and confused by the return of another teammate.

"Agatha is that really you? I thought you went insane and we locked you up and I assumed Annabelle and her goons would have done the same."

Agatha began to blast sand powerful enough to cut through my metal bounds.

"Well what happened was while they were busy tracking you down after you escaped, they forgot about the old crazy lady. I had completely left because I hated all of you and was going to wash my hands of the whole thing. Figure out a way to return to my bone fort. I was stopped in my tracks only because I heard Annabelle betrayal and truth and I might hate you, you don't deserve to go out like that at least my lover died a hero. Now let's go I have a plan."

I let out a big sigh and leaned against the pole. I ran my good fingers through my hair.

"Agatha I really appreciate you coming back for you and you having this redemption ark there is no point in escaping again. All that will happen is we fight bad guys our friends die and then we get captured by someone else. I might as well stay here and wallow in my self-pity. I rubbed my wounded wrist and huffed as I sat down once again."

"Catalyst."

"No Agatha I use to be so good at everything, I thought I knew everything about everything. Good and evil, black and white, hope and drive are not all cut and dry I use to be some dumb Gullible Wannabe hero. Now I know Zadok was right all this time, accept your current surroundings because sometimes they are the best you are going to get. Life sucks and then you die. Success is a prologue to further failure. Most of all if you do escape and fight you kill them before they can kill you. Goodbye Agatha maybe you still have time to get to safety if they don't know you escaped."

"Catalyst you can't give up, not after all we've been through. I know how you feel I thought I lost everything because of you. If I gave up and if you give up now, then Gabriel and everyone else will have died for nothing. Zadok is not right, life is not worth living if you have nowhere to go nothing to look forward to. We made a promise long ago to get off the world and stop the UN and that president guy." Said Agatha"

I thought about all the things we discussed and everything that had happened to us. Once again, I decided I would not give up without a fight. I'll get my revenge on Annabelle and fight until my last breath. I would have to change because everything I had done before let to me ultimately losing. From then on, I would do whatever it takes to win, and I would have to be willing to kill people before they could kill me. Do what needed to be done.

"Alright let's do it, For Gabriel and the people of Earth, maybe I will come out of this a better man. so, Agatha what's the plan."

She tossed me two small syringes of dark purple liquid. "If they didn't look for me because they didn't know I had left what if they are busy hallucinating to notice we are gone?" Said Agatha.

I stabbed the syringes deep into the chest of both men until their eyes glowed yellow and they passed out into the floor in a hallucinogenic state. Agatha took their Thermal guns and I took their Dark red swords.

When slipped through the door and into the dimly lit hallway. A guard started walking toward us and he must have heard our loud ass footsteps because he drew his gun and began scanning the hallway. Agatha's mouth dropped as slit his chest open and watched as his entrails were poisoned and pickled and he collapsed to the floor.

"Catalyst what the hell are you doing! You didn't have to kill that guy!"

"Now there is no chance he can kill me or any of my friends. One last guy to fight later."

She looked startled and almost afraid, she had no more to say. We came to a fork in the hallway Agatha started to walk towards the left and I to the right.

"Hey, the prison cells are this way, that's where our friends will still be," Said Annabelle.

"Exactly I'd they stay locked in their cells then they should be safe when we do what I am about to do. We are incredibly outnumbered the only way to do this with minimal deaths of our friends. Is to open the Zoo and let the creatures kill the Cardinals.

"Hey Catalyst, that sounds like a great plan and all, don't you think our escape was pretty easy what if they want you to release them to kill all of us to better harness our powers?"

"What if they want us to not release them and to do nothing. I say we start to kill e single one of them and then figure out however Annabelle can write fate and use it to free us and steal this ship and go home."

I stole the outlaw's uniform to blend in better and then maybe I could say I caught Agatha sneaking out. I heard the screams and howls of the Fermenters and other beast from beyond the door.

"Maybe you're right and we should go rescue the others first," I said.

When Agatha didn't respond I turned around to check on her, she was gone.

"Aaaaaaaaah" I heard someone scream from up ahead, so I ran toward the sound. I drew my sword and lunged at a shadowy figure and slid the blade onto their thin neck.

"Hey Catalyst, relax man it me, it's Toni. Agatha and Reuben helped us escape. Agatha sandblasted the guard and Reuben's restraints. Then Reuben liquefied Our restraints and then we simply slipped out.

I slapped Toni right across his face loud enough for the sound to echo in the hall.

"Dude what the fuck was that for "

"I wanted to make sure you were real I have been deceived this whole time. Now I have a plan on how to…" I stopped talking when I heard footsteps approaching. I tossed Toni my spare sword from David and we leaned against the wall. A large group of guards rushed past us to recapture James and the others.

"Toni, I know what the plan has to be. We must do the classic divide and conquer. Well send a couple people to get our weapons, a group to fight and hold off the outlaws and another to figure out Annabelle's Pierre and how to stop it from keeping us here."

Toni looked at me as if he agreed also questioned the logistical disadvantage of splitting up our team.

"Toni throughout history, dividing and conquering works sometimes, most of the time it epically fails. We are not the Roman Empire while we are doing all of this; you are the odd man out what will you be doing?

I swung my sword underhand and slammed it into the Cardinal's knee cap.

"Aahahah" I drove the blade into the man's neck, and his body crumbled to the floor. I reached for another man's leg and attempted to poison him when a third man kicked me in the face, and I fell to the floor. Toni pulled him off me and slammed him to the floor Toni blocked a blade attack from David, who swung a sword at my neck. We because outnumbered until James, Willard, and the others arrived.

One last swing of my sword and stabbed my sword into another Cardinals shoulder and pinned him to the floor.

"Catalyst Go, now!" James Said. he dug a blood sickle deep into. Man's back. DOOM. Willard took several metal slivers in the shoulder.

Agatha and Reuben were running to get to the vault where the outlaws were holding Toni's sword and Zadok's Amulet. The rest of my friends were attempting to hold back the Cardinals while I ran to the zoo. I grabbed a stray Thermal gun from the man I killed and used it to blast through metal door to the cells of the beast.

I heard heavy breathing and growling as I entered the familiar hallway.

This is either one of the best ideas I have ever had or by far the worst. In the distance I could still hear the clanking of swords and the blasting of guns, muffled only by screams.

I placed my hand upon the glass cell and peered at the pair of fermenters that lay inside the cell. I watched them for a moment and remembered that I killed almost their entire species or at least that pack we fought. What if I let them out and they try to kill me? Perhaps I should start with the dinosaur man and then he could talk to the Fermenter beast to beast. I knocked gently on the dinosaur man's cell. For a moment he looked like Gabriel or Willard with the sharp pointed crest, dark skin and pointed claws. I had also had a significant role in killing almost all his people. Perhaps I am the villain I am the bad guy. I have killed hundreds upon hundreds of people and now I must come to the last remnants of their species to ask for their help.

TAP, TAP, TAP. I knocked on the class until the Dinosaur man came close to the glass. His eyes pierced my own as he stared into my soul. The man spoke with a deep almost un under-stable growl.

"I was told about you Catalyst, you're the one responsible for killing all of my friends. All the men and women that arrived on this planet and helped me survivor for years and you killed them.

"No! They were not innocent! They were holding my friends and I captured and tortured us you are the villains!" I screamed.

"Mr. Catalyst a wise man once said good is a point of view and don't forget that everyone is the hero of their own story. What could you possibly have to offer me or us to help you? Your friends are probably dying right now."

"No sir, my friends are tough I do not regret killing the people that were torturing them. You can hate me you can love me I don't care we don't have to be friends, I need you and you need me. If you fight the Cardinals and hold back Annabelle while we can escape, I will break you guys out of here and I will give you enough blood to turn you human again like Ehud was able to."

"It is a deal then."

I placed the thermal gun against the glass and heated it up until it burst and shattered. Glass rained down onto the floor. The dinosaur man raised from the floor and towered over me. We turned to release the fermenters when the dinosaur man turned to me and said "My name is Nikola I was named after the great inventor Nikola Tesla.

While Nikola talked to the Fermenters, I drew the sword across my arm and as the door to the fermenters cage was opened Nikola absorbed some of my blood which allowed him to turn almost completely human. I stumbled and struggled to stand.

"Let's go kill some bad guys, you guys fight the army we will me and my crew will go for Annabelle and figure out her powers and how to get off the ship. "

My Thermal gun had over heated from being overused so much and had begun to melt in my hands. So, we set off to regroup with my friends. Nikola took the lead followed by a slow walking me and the fermenters. Who were even bigger than the ones we face outside Agatha's camp? This pair was bigger than the dog sized ones. These ones were almost as big as grizzly bears.

"Catalyst help we are being overrun we need you!" Screamed Zadok and Willard.

The first Cardinal was bitten in the neck by the fermenter the others watched in horror as his entire body was pickled and fermented as his skin turned black and purple and the Fermenters ripped him apart in seconds as if they had not eaten in weeks. They leaped from enemy to enemy seeping their claws deep into the flesh and Sucked the oxygen out and turned the sugars into carbon dioxide. Agatha and Reuben have returned with Zadok's Gauntlet, I guess Annabelle had stolen Toni's sword first because it was still missing.

"Guys let's move! Nikola, the Fermenters and the others have it under control. I tossed one of the Exploding flowers at the Cardinals that were hidden behind cover.

We rush toward the bridge and Annabelle. We would stop anywhere along the way for any clues we could use for figuring our Annabelle's power and how it was keeping us from leaving the planet.

"Catalyst let me get this straight your fiancé betrayed you and ultimately wants to use your powers and ours to take over the world in a government coup and you turn around and put all your faith it random strangers who you have never met before and that you killed all of their friends and that could easily kill you ." Said Zadok.

"Yes, pretty much, Agatha taught me even the worst things in the world can be forgive and if not forgiven then at least put aside until a point when our goal is reached like getting home. For the record I don't trust them at all. After getting betrayed by Annabelle I don't trust anyone except James. I think they are going to betray us, you know what we needed them, and so I took that gamble. "

Chapter twenty-one

"Damn its Catalyst where is my sword? E time we get free from these fucking prisons my sword is stolen." Said Toni

We were headed toward the bridge and could still hear the screams of cardinals being shredded and rotted by fermenters.

"Toni, Zadok I got it! So, with your Amulet you can bring through weapons that people in your bloodline have touched. Does that include you? "

Zadok stopped in his tracks and turned toward Toni before activating his amulet. His eyes glowed golden and he pulled out a Falcata sword like what Toni's sword was.

"There Toni I know it's not exact that's not how it works. It takes a lot more than me touching it for me to be able to pull it through the amulet. Maybe sometimes I will explain to you how it works. Until then I think it would be best to focus on the mission at hand."

For a while we walked in silence and spoke only when we would come across a guard that we would have to fight. E time we would argue whether it was necessary to kill them.

"Catalyst you do not have to kill them! If you can trust that random dinosaur man, then why can you not spare an outlaw. Is it because they work for the women who betrayed you," Said Agatha?

"Yes, maybe, I don't know look Agatha after Gabriel I don't think we should waste our time fighting."

"Guys shut the hell up, she's going to hear us coming for twenty minutes." Said James

"Well of this ship is as big as I think it is and judging by how many Mercenaries or Cardinals or outlaws whatever the hell they are called this ship must be a fortress like the size of several aircraft carriers not to mention it's a high tech spaceship obviously they have cameras and sensors she's probably playing with us mocking with us." Said Willard.

I heard the click of an intercom turning on and then a muffled voice.

"You know you're all quite right there is such thing as being too smart for your own good." Said Annabelle.

Over the intercom I heard her scribbling frantically in her notebook.

"You wanted a way off of this planet and I've decided maybe it's best if I let you go after all I don't have to wait for you to be dead to harness your powers all I need is your blood "

Panels in the wall slid back and several red robotic like drone men lunged and tried to grab us.

I tried to poison them obviously it didn't work because they were robots and Annabelle knew I wouldn't be able to. James sickle landed a solid blow deep to the robot's chest as he ripped the robot chest open and blasted a thermal gun into his chest. Zadok pulled a Katana out of his amulet and chopped a robot arm off. Willard dug his claws into one of the robot's chest before the drone blasted him in the face with his own type of acid.

"aaaa what the actual fucking hell" Willard screamed before passing out.

"James, I need a weapon!" I screamed

He strained himself and his energy he was able to produce a Gladius I tried to stab the drone and began to drag my blade down the back of the robot when it shifted and turned into a flying drone before spraying my face with a purplish gas . I felt an incredibly sharp pain and stab deep in my back. My body seized up and I must have been temporarily paralyzed because I could not fight or even move. I glanced to the other side of the room and I saw Agatha blasting the robots with sand and rocks while Toni sliced them with his Falcata. The drone blasted Agatha with flames until her sand heated to glass and shot back at her lodging deep in her skin.

My eyes flickered and closed as they had so many times before the last thing, I saw was my friends all get pierced with Gigantic needles.

I managed to only get out a few mumbles before the drones knocked us out.

When I awoke the seven of my friends and I were all strapped into chairs into what I could only guess was an escape pod of sorts. The seats were all back to back and the controls ran along the wall around us. In the doorway stood Annabelle who held seven large quarts of blood cradled in her arms.

"Catalyst you wanted off the planet and I am giving you your wish.as the president sent you a way to get you out of the way I am sorry, I must do the same. Now that I have your blood, I will utilize your power as many have tried to do before. I'll go back to Earth and take it over while you guys get shot into space with enough fuel to strand you in space. Goodbye Catalyst I cannot have you intervening or compromising my power."

I opened my mouth to respond she began to shut the door. She blew me a kiss and the door hissed closed. We were forced to wait and listen to the sound of the engine of Annabelle's ship lift off away from the planet where we had spent almost a year of our lives and go through so much. For a year all I ever thought about was getting off that damn planet and now that we were, I would have given anything to have stayed. Once her ship was pushed through the planet's atmosphere and gravitational pull. I heard an incredibly loud noise as our escape pod was shot into deep space with as little fuel as possible.

The further away from the planet we drifted the dimmer the lights inside our pod became as it tried to push the life support if it could.

"Catalyst I know we have gotten out of tough spots before how are we going to get out of this one man. How do we beat someone who can affect everything? We have no Fuel or Food or anything! I wish we were back on the planet eating plants and drinking that purple water," James screamed as he pounded his fist into the control panel in front of him. The lights dimmed ever further until we could barely see anything in the pod except for the light of the control panels.

"James if there is one thing, we found out on this journey it is that we are determined to survive we will find the way," I said.

"There is a way, one way. If you kill me Catalyst, then Reuben could make fuel from my body like he did with the dinosaur men. Then you guys could make it back to Earth," Said Toni.

From where I was sitting, I could only see Zadok, Agatha and Reuben.

"No Toni there is always another way we have to work it out. I cannot lose another friend especially one I have to kill. What if Reuben can somehow use my Poison or a weapon from Zadok's Amulet to make fuel from."

Zadok's fingers curled tightly around his amulet as he stared into the darkness. His beard had grown long and scraggly and he looked like a grey Jesus.

"Catalyst most metals contain only a trace amount of hydrogen or oxygen, besides the fact that we need heat to create energy and the explosion that creates the force that pushes the ship forward. This is it Catalyst we are done, this is the end of our story," Said Zadok.

"No Zadok you shut the fuck up, I laid down and tried to give up once because of you and because I felt betrayed and whined like a child and I will not do it again. You're right about the hydrogen from metal being sparse there is plenty in certain venoms …" I said.

It was getting harder and harder to breath as the room faded to almost complete darkness and with it out faded almost all hope. I reached over and slid my fingers across Agatha's palm until they rested in between her fingers. I tried to force out a whisper, my sentences came out broken and quiet.

"Agatha there is oxygen in sand, and there is hydrogen in certain venoms I have to do it through touch what if you start blasting sand while I fill it with poison on top of the sand then Reuben could break it apart and make fuel. There are only a few minutes left and I know it's a crazy long shot, we only have time for one and if it doesn't work, we will be to dead to care anyway," I said.

Agatha squeezed my hand and I felt it feel with sand. I began to produce a low toxic venom on top of the sand.

"Reuben get ready to break the elements and produce the fuel, Willard can produce heat by melting his outer restraints with acid," I said.

The room faded to complete darkness with even the control panels ceasing to produce light. Everyone in the room began to take quick rapid breaths as I felt my lungs struggle to capture oxygen my lungs and throat tighten as I took my last breath and my eyes began to close.

BOOM! The escape pod shook violently as a blinding light filled the cabin and air filled our lungs. Reuben was still breathing hard due to his

Exasperation of energy. We finally had begun to breathe easy when the ship began to spiral out of control.

"Toni can you fly this ship?" Willard asked

The ship jerked in the opposite directions as Toni tugged at the lever in front of him.

"Fly I cannot, we probably won't crash I definitely Can keep us from dying maybe. In the least I can guide us to Earth." Said Toni.

"James plot a course, I believe the Navigation panel is in front of you," screamed Zadok.

I glanced out of the window as we blasted through the cosmos until the Earth finally came into view days later. Throughout the entire day long journey, I felt my stomach digest itself. I felt the hunger eat away at the inside of my throat. The second the Earth came into view all thoughts of food and worry, pain and hunger, loss and betrayal faded. Completely replaced with thoughts of joy, wonder and the return of hope.

We approached Earth's upper atmospheric and fell even faster. Toni and James attempted to reverse our thrusters to slow the pod down so we would not crash and die.

My face began to burn and then my neck and chest until my entire body felt as if I was laying at the bottom of a frying pan. The inside of the ship grew hotter and hotter while Our escape pod's Ablative shields struggled to protect us from the heat. I heard the metal bend and crack before the bolts popped out like fireworks. Which in turn blasted holes into the wall of the ship due to the immense pressure.

"Catalyst what are we supposed to do, what the heck is the point of surviving everything if we die right here," Said Agatha

"No, we will survive we always do," I said.

I was so sure we would that I didn't notice the entire wall in front of Toni ripped off and got sucked into the atmosphere. He stabbed his sword into the floor of the ship and held onto the hilt with everything he had.

"Toni hold on! Reuben stop the fuel and melt my restraints" I screamed

I looked Agatha in her eyes and had to let go of her hand so that's I could reach for Toni while I also held on to my seat belt and Agatha held my waist.

"Catalyst here take this!" Zadok screamed and his eyes glowed the familiar gold and he pulled a metal staff from his amulet and passed it around the cabin until I could grab it. After that our decent toward the Earth surface was a blur and I only remember fragments.

The pressure tried to suck us out into the atmosphere, the noise of the wind and air rushing around us the heat began to melt the edges of the hole in the pod. Toni's sword slipped and he started to be sucked into the air. He grabbed into the staff and I tried to pull him inside when I began to be sucked out too. Agatha and James pulled me inside along with Toni. By the time we settled down into our seats though I saw ground approaching.

"Reuben give me the ring now!" Said Agatha

He tossed her the ring and she slipped it on her finger. The rings band glowed green and her eyes turned grey and she blasted powerful sand out of the open side of the pod.

The blast hit the ground and it turned it into dense quicksand. The ship let out on last whistle of air and then a loud BOOM as it slammed into the quicksand. The escape pod shook violently, and my head slammed into the wall and I fell unconscious.

I must have been passed out for hours because when I awoke it was dark again and the lighting in what was left of the escape pod was dim. The floor was broken, and some parts were completely missing all together. The roof had collapsed where the wall had been torn away in front of Toni.

My eyes we're having trouble adding to the difference of pressure and composition of the Earth's atmosphere from …the other planet. It was in that moment I realized we lived on a planet for a year and we never named it. While I was distracted by my thoughts, I failed to notice I had landed in Agatha's lap. We exchanged awkward glances as I bolted up straight before doubling over in excruciating Pain.

I snapped awake once again and I had to shake myself to stay awake. My eyes had finally added to the pressure when I glanced to the outside world and by eyes were blasted once again with bright blinding colors. I almost forgot how beautiful the world really is. Everyone takes everything for granted even being able to see a world in color. I stood up to check on my friends and see the blue sky and e other color in the world when my legs collapsed from under me and I landed on my ass.

"God damn it I really hope this is because of a change in the gravity fields and not because of a loss in bone density," I whispered to Agatha.

"Can you walk Catalyst; we need to recon and figure out where we are and maybe find some damn food we haven't eaten in forever." Said Agatha.

"Tell me about it dude I almost started to chew Zadok's fingers off. Don't you guys think we should check on the others before we venture out?"

"James" Agatha and I screamed in unison.

Tap. Tap. Tap. Click.

"Fuck why won't this crap work" Zadok said as he poked the keyboard and began slamming his fist into the keyboard and screen in front of him.

"This computer won't turn on; we don't know where we are and we're all starving! We probably have bone density loss. I haven't walked in Earth's gravity in like a hundred years. How the fuck are we supposed to walk who the hell knows how long and then battle a damn super villain and her army," Said Zadok

"Hey Zadok, how about you stop your damn whining all you do is be negative all the time. No matter how many times we succeed and get over e obstacle your still so damn negative." Screamed Toni.

They began to scream at each other until my ears began to ring and ring.

"Shut the HELL UP I can't even hear myself think. I am going to go for a walk and figure out where we are. Maybe by the time I get back you guys can get along and stop arguing like children. THERE IS SO MUCH AT STAKE HERE!" I screamed.

I attempted to stand my legs were to weak and I fell back into my seat. I pressed my left hand into the inner thighs of my right leg. I had to force myself to lift my leg and place it further along the floor. I lifted my legs again and again. I looked down and saw the staff from Zadok and pulled myself up with the staff leaning all my weight into the metal rod. The metal staff clanked loudly against the broken floor of the escape pod.

I shuffled to the end of the metal platform using the staff as a walking stick. The sky was a brilliant beautiful blue. I forgot how sweet the air was and tasted almost a crisp Clean feeling. It was then that was probably the nicest moment of them all. I felt a cold breeze blow across my face, and it did cut me.

I took one small step and for the first time in a year my foot landed on the Earth's surface. I walked with the staff drinking in my surroundings. I turned around and, in the distance, I saw quick movement into the distance. I hobbled across a clearing as fast as I could. My ears began to drown in the rushing of sound, and I saw and hear what the movement was. Thousands of gallons of water gushing over a waterfall. I felt a deep rumble in my legs as the ground shook. I knew where we had crashed, Niagara Falls. About 500 miles from the UN headquarters in New York City.

Chapter twenty-two

I hobbled as fast as I could over to the edge of the river and dropped my face into the water and lapping up as much as I could. I sat up and raised my cupped hand to my lips and drank until my stomach was bursting with water. I pulled myself up on my staff and continued to walk. For what felt like hours on end I stood at the edge of the falls starring deep into the rushing water. The water thundered in my ears while the white foam spilled over the rocks. It was as if this was the calm before the storm and we were in for one last brutal hurricane. I was so entranced by the water fall I failed to hear someone walk up behind me. I looked up to see Reuben standing a foot or two behind me holding what appeared to be a cloth grocery store sack. He reached in and pulled out a granola bar and tossed it to me. I put into it and it tasted as if it expired twenty years ago. The crazy thing about food is when you haven't eaten in two weeks even ridiculously stale food taste amazing.

"Reuben thank you so much where the hell did you find this stuff?" I asked

Reuben looked at me and for only about the second time since I've known him, he opened his mouth to speak. His voice was jagged and harsh as if rough and unpracticed.

"A few miles away there is an abandon grocery store I grabbed a few of these sacs of supplies I figured it will be a long walk to New York."

He stopped talking as fast as he had started before bending down to fill a metal water bottle with water.

My legs were getting stronger with each step I took I hoped in time I would be able to walk without the staff.

Hours had passed before Reuben and I finally made it back to the others. I heard a low familiar hum coming from beyond the twists frame of the escape pod. Besides that, it was silent, no screaming, and no fighting. Peace.

"Hello guys, were back. We're at Niagara Falls so we've got a long journey ahead of us." I said

"Well Catalyst that's why we spent the time you were gone building this," Toni screamed.

from behind the remnants of my escape pod came the others.

"Presenting the cosmic carriage 2" Said Zadok

It was similar to the first cosmic carriage they built all that time ago, except even better and more secure because they used the beams and metal from escape pod. The carriage was black and silver with red beams. The thrusters were even larger on the second carriage.

"Well guess we mind as we'll get going then." I said.

We climbed into the carriage and closed the doors shut behind us. The Carriage moves faster and faster across the green countryside. Narrowly avoiding trees and marvel we zoomed from town to town. Toni and Zadok took the front of the carriage and James and I guarded the back. We joked around made small talk, ate expired snacks, and drank fresh cool river water.

"Hey Catalyst, check the tree line to the north east. "said James.

My eyes scanned the horizon and the locked on to a familiar black outfit. They came into focus and I could tell it was a large patrol of men.

I saw the familiar red and black of the Cardinals uniform. There was about two dozen men in tight rows all with a thermal blaster and sword. Led by that crazy Indian guy from before. I think his names was Harsh. I ran my fingers over the fresh burned scars in my back that were compliments of him.

"I say we wait here and ambush them, maybe capture one and question them until they give us information on Annabelle's whereabouts and everything else." I said.

"Catalyst your too soft I say we take out have of them by running them the hell over. Kill all the stranglers. Guess what none of them are going to talk anyway you said it yourself. Kill them before they can kill us," Said Zadok

He rubbed the amulet through his fingers once again. His eyes turned gold as they usually do this time the veins in his face flashed gold and black.

"Zadok are you alright?" I asked. The mercenary's foot fall grew closer and closer.

"when I use to go adventuring, I would use the amulets power maybe twice a year. Then I was without it for fifty. In the past year however I've been using it almost daily and it's killing me. Look a Reuben's rings it's been constant in use since I pulled it through time like eight months ago so no I am not alright."

"I'm so sorry man I had no idea! Dude take away this stupid staff I've been using as a cane and take away the ring!"

Zadok released the staff to the Amulet and put his hand out for Reuben to return the ring. Reuben raised his hands and the hesitated unwilling to return the power enhancer. Zadok was getting frustrated I could tell I stood up and his brow furrowed.

"Guys whatever is going on is going to have to wait. If we are going to fight, we're going to have to stop here if we want any cover." Yelled James.

The carriage stopped suddenly, and my head was thrown forward almost hitting the seat in front of me.

"We might have cover we're short on long range weapons, only things I can think of would be my sand blast and if James could make a spear of some sort…"

DOOM, DOOM, DOOM TSSSS. The carriage was already starting to take blast from the cardinals' guns. The seven of us were all huddled together behind the turned over carriage. Sweat was pouring down my forehead and stinging my eyes. With each hit from the blasters the carriage grew hotter and hotter as the metal started to melt.

"Now or never, Agatha give me your hand!"

I reached over and laid my hand barely on top of hers. We stood up and she blasted poisoned sand into the first row of outlaws. The blast of sand was so powerful it would knock the soldiers back while bruising and cutting their skin until the poison killed them.

James cut himself and was about to form a weapon when Toni shouted. "James the Spears of the Native American tribe the Tohono O'odham were small enough so you could make several while also having distance of a spear.!" Toni shouted. James got to work hardening his blood and making more Spears.

"Willard take Toni and Reuben and try to flank them, the rest of us will stay here and lay down cover fire." I said.

By that time the army of mercenaries was only a few feet away and Agatha and I were growing tired and exhausted. Agatha collapsed and slumped down next to Zadok, I reached down to place my finger on her neck as I checked for a pulse.

“Give up Catalyst while you still have some dignity, or you will all die here and now as no ones in this shitty field “said Harsh.

“No Harsh I think it’s you who should surrender before you all die, you think you have us surrounded it’s the other way around. Guys now!” I screamed

James threw a small spear into the man standing next to Harsh and he feel dead.

“Catalyst is right Harsh no one else has to die, tell your men to drop their weapons and well keep you all as prisoners.” Said James

Harsh turned around fast enough to let off a single shoot before diving to the floor.

“Fuck! That was my good arm!” James screamed as he too passed out from shock. The thermal blast has taken out a decent sized chunk of his good arm. Willard attempted to douse the ground in acid to melt the sand enough to capture some of Harsh’s men without killing them.

“Hello dumbass they have no problem killing us so why not kill them first!” Zadok screamed. His legs wobbled as he struggled to stand, using the melted metal from the carriage as support.

Click click click. I heard the familiar sound of guns reloading as the army got ready to charge.

“You had your chance Catalyst now your blood will be ours as well as the death of millions being your fault. “said Harsh. He drew his familiar red sword before raising it into the air. He took two steps forward before yelling "Charge!" Some of his men drew their swords while others drew a second gun. They began to jog and then run towards us screaming with their weapons raised in the air.

"You won't take my blood this time Ehud! "Reuben screamed. He ran forward surprising the outlaws and threw his hands into the dirt at their feet.

"No one will ever take my blood again!" Reuben screamed as he turned the sand into liquid sand and the Cardinals began to sink deep into the liquid sand.

"Reuben this is not you and they are not Ehud you do not have to do this these are not monsters these are men, if you do this then you will be a monster" I said.

"I already am"

He bent down and touched the liquefied sand again turning it back into a solid.

"Aaaa what the fuck!"

I heard the loudest screams I have ever heard in my entire like. I heard the crushing of chest, snapping of bones and the loud exhale as e ounce of air and life was forced out of their bodies. Some men killed themselves if they feared a slow death.

Reuben walked over to the few men whose bodies were crushed with their chest above the sand and grabbed a sword before walking away as if nothing happened.

"If they were here, they must have a ship nearby we should find it and then head to New York." Said Reuben

My eyes locked onto Willard's and we exchanged wide eyes troubled glances. The returned to where we stood, they walked across the field of various lifeless body parts jutting out from the sand like stalagmites on a cave floor.

I helped Agatha to her feet while James hardened the bloody hole in this arm while coagulating the wound. I tore off my jacket is and fastened a sling for James's arm. We started to walk

"Reuben that wasn't ok you had them trapped you did not have to kill them; we could have gotten important statistics on battle tactics and how many soldiers they have!" I said.

"Catalyst that sounds hypocritical when we were on the cardinal's ship you killed several men that you didn't have to because you felt betrayed." Said Agatha.

I opened my mouth to speak when Zadok stepped up next to Agatha and got into my face once more.

"Reuben was seriously psychologically messed up so messed up he didn't speak. Harsh uttered the same line Ehud said e day when he ripped blood from our flesh. I would have done the same thing and you know what I think you're mad there's no one left to tell you where your girlfriend is." Said Zadok

"You know it's not like that I think we should try to be heroes again if we really want to save the world. "I said.

"Well guess what Catalyst we've been through all of this before because we have powers does not make us heroes."

I swung and my fist connected with Zadok's jaw he turned and tried to shove me.

"ENOUGH let's go search for the ship, Catalyst maybe the problem is you we were getting along while building the carriage in your absence. Perhaps we should all walk in silence for a while." Said Willard

That was exactly what we did, we walked in silence for over an hour. We combed through what woods remained around Niagara Falls until we came across an empty clearing. I picked up a rock and chucked it into the center of the clearing. THUD. The rock appeared to float above the ground by a dozen feet or so.

"guessing this is some sort of cloaked plane or ship." I said

"Well if it's cloaked how are we supposed to board or fly it?" Asked James. Before anyone could answer Agatha has started to blast the area under the rock with sand. The sand gave us an idea of how big the plane was, it appeared to be an armored and weaponized commercial jet.

Willard stepped forward and placed his hand flat against invisible ship. Black acid began to ooze from his hand and run down the wall of sand and dropped to the floor with a sizzling hiss.

"Reuben May I have the ring? There seems to be some sort of shielding on it and my acid is not strong enough to burn through it.

Maybe with the ring it will boost my powers enough to get us through, said Willard.

Reuben walked over to where Willard and Agatha were standing and curled his fingers around his ringed fingers and plunged it into his pocket.

"No, you do not need the ring, the ring is mine."

Reuben pushed his hands through the wall of sand until the metal shook and bubbles before falling to the floor in a puddle of metal and sand. He only melted the wall closet to us so that the rest of the ship was still whole and cloaked. It appeared to be a window into a ship in the middle of an empty field. We all began to step forward and into the ship one at a time. Surprisingly there was only two guards about Reuben has one foot in the door when Zadok places his hand upon his shoulder and whispered

"Thanks for the help I really am going to need that ring back bud."

Reuben tried to twist out of Zadok's grasp Zadok dug his fingers into his shoulders even tighter.

He tried to pull and tug on Reuben's arm and hand, Reuben turned and shoved his hand into Zadok's chest.

The old man tumbled out of the door and into the sand.

"Uh Zadok I'm sorry"

He attempted to put his hand out to help Zadok to his feet Zadok slapped his hand away.

"Whatever forget about it give me the damn ring ass hole."

Reuben have him the dirtiest look I have ever seen someone give to another person and he dropped the ring unto Zadok's chest with a metallic *plink.*

Zadok stood to his feet and pushed the ring back into the amulet.

We began to explore the jet there was not much to it. A cockpit with the pilot and copilot seat along with the controls, two rows of dozens of seats, and the back of the plane made up a giant prison cell. As far as weapons go, the Cardinal's jet has a gun turret mounted to each side of the plane and a middle launcher built into the nose.

Toni and I walked toward the front of the ship while the others took seats in various parts of the main cabin. Instead of being a unified team like we needed to be we were a group of people who happened to share a common hatred and a need for survival. I once thought we could make a great family right now, I can't even see us being friends.

"Hey Toni, can you even fly this kind of plane?"

"Yes, sir I can fly almost any plane or helicopter, let's not forgotten I even kind of flew that escape pod."

"Oh, that's right I forgot you were in the military, which branch was it again?"

"Catalyst I am one of the only people to be in e branch of the military, at one point or another I even served in about e special op team there ever was, want to be my copilot?"

I jumped into the copilot seat and glanced over e ton, switch, and lever.

"Toni I would love to, as long as you make sure I know how to fly this kind of jet haha."

Reuben reached out of the plane and dipped his fingers into the liquefied metal. The metal hardened into solid steel once again. We set a course for New York City and began the small flight.

Chapter twenty-three

For the first hour of the flight the only noise we heard was the low hum of the jet's engines. The plane was still relatively quiet, no one Said or did anything except awkwardly stare at each other. I started to return to the cabin when I heard noises coming from behind me.

Click, Click Dum Dum dum. I heard a heavy machine gun firing and reloading again and again.

"Who the hell is trying to let e bad guy in New York know we are coming!" I screamed

The door to the turret opened and I saw Agatha step out.

"Agatha what the hell are you thinking besides hurting innocent people you're going to alert everyone in the city!"

"Well guess what Catalyst, were in fucking New York where your psycho ass Girlfriend is trying to enslave the world, so she probably knows where here. Hello, she is damn puppet master. She can literally help make certain things happen I'm sure we are only here because she wants us to be." Said Agatha.

"Agatha while I understand what you're saying I really do think we should hold off on the signal flares ok "

"Fine"

"Hey Catalyst, I think you better get up here!" Said Toni from the cockpit.

I hesitantly entered the cockpit knowing that we were all about to be in a bad way once again. As if me trying to avoid it would make it not happen.

Ksssssh pop hiss. The radio began to crackle and hiss before breaking in and out. It was then I heard a familiar sound that was once comforting has become eerie. The radio became clear and the only sound that could be heard was the scribbling of a pen feverishly flying across a page. the pen screeched to a halt followed by the pucker of a wax seal.

"Once again my love, your fate has been written and sealed." Said Annabelle over the radio.

Click. The radio went dead once again, and the jet grew silent. Toni and I exchanged worried glances.

"Catalyst, what are we supposed to do? how do we prepare for something we don't know? We have to go tell the others."

"Toni we can't be ready because I think we won't have to wait long to find out. Fine I'll go tell them right now."

I stood up to find James and the others and to update them on Annabelle's chilling penman ship. However, before I could exit the cabin Agatha cane running in screaming.

"Guys there is smoke coming from the tail end of the plane and the one of the engine has caught on fire .What the hell are we supposed to do and what's going to stop Annabelle from writing someone else if wc gct out of this .?" Agatha asked.

I stared into Agatha's face for a moment before answering then I glanced out the window at the trail of grey smoke we were now leaving. I ran my hands through my crusty and sand filled hair to focus harder and come up with a somewhat decent plan. I pushed the door open so the others sitting in the cabin heard me.

"Stop me if I'm wrong guys from what I understand about Annabelle's powers, besides having to be written by her in her book. She can only help things that could happen otherwise she would have had us kill ourselves or each other," I said.

"Catalyst thanks for that keen observation time to talk is done we need to act before we spin out of control." Said Zadok

I watched the radio altimeter as our altitude dropped.

"That's it! Agatha if we get to the right altitude where the cabin pressure is equal to the surrounding air, we can open the emergency door and you can put the fire out with sand." I said

“That’s the stupidest idea I have ever heard the chances of that are slim to none, I say we crash land and if we survive walk the rest of the way. “Yelled Zadok.

We all found our seats and buckled up. Agatha began to blast the emergency door with sand with bigger and bigger blast until the door busted open. I grabbed unto Agatha waist and held her tight and she attempted to lean out of a moving plane. She attempted to coat the fire with a thick layer of sand, yet the fire would not extinguish.

I heard the air begin to be sucked from the cabin as the plane started into a barrel roll. At first Agatha and I were pulled out into the air as I frantically latched o. To a dangling seat belt. I felt my heart pounding through my chest and on the side of my head. When we thought we were ok the plane barrel rolled again and we were thrown into the far wall of the plane.

“Cut the engines Toni the fires will stop because the fuel source will be gone, maybe we can glide into the city.” I screamed while being thrown around the plane.

Toni steadied the plane one last time and cut the engines. After a few moments the smoke lessened, and we began to glide. I pulled myself and Agatha into the seats nearest to us before buckling us in.

We glided for a few minutes before we entered the forbidden New York City airspace and we noticed something was wrong. When we had left the City was still in its beautiful former glory. Now it resembled a post-apocalyptic waste land. E building was completely missing its top half or complete gone except for the United Nations headquarters. That building was bigger and more armored than ever before. It closely resembled a castle, Ehud's castle. The other major difference was that the sky was grey along with everything else. The city had become dark and colorless like the planet we were banished to. Annabelle truly was trying to make this a darker world and she was using everything from the other planet to do so. After we had entered the city's air space, we had to finally make use of the planes weapons and Agatha finally got to use her turret to blast several robotic drones out of the sky.

We had passed over UN building and had continued gliding we had lost most of our altitude to the point that we were almost at building level.

"Toni if you come close to where those to buildings meet, I can see the Remnants of an old cable bridge perhaps we can land the plane the way the use to land planes on those old school aircraft carriers. By flying low enough to snag that cable with the plane and getting snagged to a halt. "said Willard.

"Hell, it's worth and shot, if it fails, we'll be to dead to care." Said Toni.

Toni pulled back on the wheel as far as he could which barely increased our altitude by a few feet.

The plane flew incredibly close to the narrow bride before it attempted to grab the cable continued to fly before the plane jerked to a stop. My head slammed the back of the seat and I heard an incredible metallic Thwack like when an archer releases his bow. The plane was pulled back behind the bride until the nose of the plane gridded against the bridge. While the t of the plane was pushed backwards and tore up hundreds of pounds of concrete and asphalt as it digs into the ground. Miraculously and with what seemed like sheer coincidence the plane stopped moving.

I felt lightheaded and I realized I had been holding my breath for who knows how long. I released my lock knees and pried my fingers off the seat in front of me before letting out a long deep breath of relief.

“We are going to need a base, and this isn’t it, preferably one where we can see Annabelle’s building,” I said.

“Perhaps we could hide and travel in the sewers, storm water system” Toni said as he stroked his beard.

“I haven’t been to earth in almost a hundred years, obviously a lot and happened especially in the last few years perhaps the ancient subway tunnels would be a good way of moving throughout the city with little detection.” Whispered Zadok.

“Alright that sounds like a good plan we need to do whatever it takes to get that book away from Annabelle because if we don’t, we will have no chance of victory” I said

We took one last look inside the plane for supplies or anything else that could be useful. We were about to step out when I noticed a small hatch in the floor.

James created a blood sword and sliced clean through the hinges. When he lifted the hatch, it revealed several of the thermal blaster pistols, a few red swords, also there was a few weapons we had not seen before. The new weapons included a Gatling gun type gun like the thermal guns, several melee weapons that appeared to be made from a material close to Willard's claws. An acid thrower. The last weapon was confused is at first then we realized it was a cannon that worked like slivers powers it had a big drum on top of the barrel where you loaded any material until it was able to turn it into slivers and bits of the material until it could blast them out of the barrel. We grabbed as many weapons as we could carry and exited the ship to hunt for the tunnels.

"Woah holy hell, I think I'll take that one." Said Willard

He reached down and grabbed the last remaining weapon. A large war hammer that was to be made like James's weapons. Reuben turned and places his hands in various parts of the ship. Turning each one of them into a liquid or gas so that no one could discover where we landed or where we were going.

Toni took point as always, he held a sword readied and a gun bolstered on his hip, Willard and James guarded the rear while the rest of us stayed in the middle. After a few minutes we approached a small boarded up subway entrance. There was a sign on the door that read. **Keep out by order of Director Bishop.**

Whack, whack, crack! Willard raised his war hammer and bashed through the metal and wood cover. One at a time we descended the stairs into the dark tunnel below. Once we were inside the only light was the faint light that shown through the subway entrance. We walked in silence our footsteps echoing off the tunnel walls. Several portions of the tunnels had collapsed completely, and we were forced to make twist and turns. I heard a faint dripping of water. *Plink plink plink.*

Then came a scurry of tiny feet upon the concrete floor. I glanced down and saw a millipede stop and curl itself up upon the floor. My neck hair stood on into and I brought the heel of my foot down upon the arthropod until only a puddle of goo remained.

"What you do that for?" Asked Willard

"For Gabriel"

We continued to walk along the tunnel until we saw a sliver of light. *Scratch scratch scratch* the scratching stopped and a familiar beast leaped into the tunnel. *Sniff sniff* the monster opened his mouth and the light glistened off his long sharp teeth. I cocked my thermal pistol and raised my right hand and had already started think about what poison to use. I heard the loud metallic scraping as Toni dragged his sword across the concrete floor. The creature jumped into the light and I saw the beast was a fermenter.

"What the Fuck aren't these damn things supposed to be back on the other planet!" Screamed Toni.

"We should have figured they would be here, we let them lose on Annabelle's ship remember, her silver tongue probably got them on her side." I said

The fermenter lunged attempting to bring his teeth down upon Agatha's throat, Toni brought swung his arms up and blocked the fermenters mouth with the sword. Toni was pushed into the floor and the fermenter bit down on the sword and snapped it clean in two. James threw me into the fermenter, and I brought my sword and hand into the beast chest. *Awolowo*, the fermenter Howled and screamed. He began his scratch and flail. His claw came down upon Agatha's arm and it began to become purple.

"Agatha no!" I screamed

Before I could help her, I heard the clicking and clacking of claws on the concrete floor coming towards us from the darkness.

"Agatha!"

I grabbed Agatha's arm and dragged my sword across the dark purple skin until I had removed all the rot and ferment. James reached over and coagulated and clotted her blood.

Zadok and Reuben began to blast the darkness with thermal guns until the clacking stopped. The tunnel had begun to light up from the bright blast. It wasn't one fermenter over Ten.

Willard swung his hammer and crushed one of the Fermenters back side and finally head he used the claw on the back of the hammer to rip deep into another. I pressed my fingers into the Fermenters cuts and injected him with box jellyfish toxin. He went into cardiac arrest until his heart exploded dousing me in blood and ooze.

Agatha attempted to blast them back with sand, she could only use her left hand.

James attempted to forge his famous blood sickles when a Fermenter bit his finger off, the rot began to travel up his finger.

"AAAAA HOLY FUCK I AM NOT LOSING THIS ARM TOO!" James screamed. He used his jagged arm to cut off the rotted fingertip and clotted the blood. The Fermenters kept coming and coming.

"Agatha sand wall now! Reuben try hardening the sand!"

They jumped to action and attempted to do what I asked when another fermenter jumped through the partial sand wall and jumped to the roof to escape. We all slid to the ground in exhaustion and attempted to help cover each other's room.

We began walking again when we heard a faint voice in the distance. It was an old TV, the TV was playing a continuous loop. It was Annabelle sitting behind her desk looking both evil and enchanting.

"Attention citizens surrender now, or I will be forced to bring New York to its knees with any means necessary. I will level the city it I must, stragglers will be killed." Said Annabelle

The same ten second clip repeated. How could this Psychopathic murdering super dictator be the same beautiful girl I fell in love with when we crashed on that planet over a year ago.

"There is no way she got here that long before us most of that building rubble was fresh, she must only have control of New York. Which means we could still end her Coup de ta right here and now" Toni said.

"Then we Better get out of this subway and figure out how to defeat her and get that book and set things right. I know because we have special abilities does not automatically make us superheroes, I think it wouldn't hurt to try", I said

We found a subway exit and we were able to exit to the street once we bashed open the covering. We were forced to scale the closest building because of the sheer number of troops patrolling the city. From the partially collapsed tower we saw the Unites nations building. Swarming around the sky were robotic drones and mercenaries with Gabriel like wings on their backs. Cardinals, Fermenters and dinosaur men guarded the tower at the base and on e level from e window. As for the streets surrounding the building there were dozens of giant cockroaches and millipedes. This was going to be one hell of a final battle.

Chapter twenty-four

For a while we sat at the top of the partial destroyed building we stared over the remnants of the city and thousands upon thousands of enemies. We waited on the building for hours, planning and talking and getting rest. Darkness fell upon the city and everyone began to sleep. Agatha attempted to lean against me, I pulled myself away.

"Catalyst do you think we'll be able to do it. I mean I know everyone tends to think of themselves as invincible and that they can do it. Everyone thinks of themselves as this untouchable hero when really, they are the guy the hero punches in the face. That with everything in life it always ends with the heroes wining. Life is not black and white sometimes heroes fail. Catalyst all those years I spent on that planet I was never as scared as I am now. I don't want to die Catalyst."

I looked at Agatha's face and the face of all my friends. I looked down upon the street and saw the glimmer of the light upon the shells of the insects. The scurrying of millions of feet upon the concrete streets. I paused and thought deeply about what I said next and what we would do next.

"Agatha my entire life has been defined constantly fighting, battle after battle. It never gets any easier, you never stop being afraid of dying. I think that is perhaps what villains have that we don't. They are not afraid to fight, hurt, and be killed. It gives them strength. I think fear is a good thing, when you become fearless people tend to do stupid things. However, the thought never crossed my mind that we won't when, it's not a question of If we win, when. Good always wins in the end the only variable is at what cost." I said.

Scratch scratch scratch. I stood up to see what was making the strange noise and I found Toni carving symbols into the floor with a sword.

"Catalyst I have been up all night, running through hundreds of battle tactics and strategies. The best I can figure it if we sweep in and attack each separate group and cut them off from the rest of her army. It will be easier than any head on approach. We simply do not have enough people to do a sweeping envelopment and in order to fake retreat we would have to attack them head in first. We know their weaknesses Catalyst as long as we still have the element of surprise, ambushing them is our best bet."

We made it the ground level of the tower and we explored for the best vantage point of the streets and buildings surrounding Annabelle's United Nations tower.

"I think it would be best if some of us stayed here in case something bad happens we won't all be captured," Said Toni

We all nodded in agreement as we gazed upon each other's faces. We tried to read one another, and I could tell everyone was worried. In all the battles we had before their worry was there, it was never this bad. Everyone is so tired and physically and mentally exhausted. Zadok began to fidget and pace across the floor.

"Guys I don't get it why the hell are we doing this! We are back on Earth; I am back on Earth after a hundred years. What are we doing? Fighting a powerful villain with an army that will probably cause the death of most of us. Even if we defeat her then we get to spend years fighting the president and his army that covers the fucking globe. What are we supposed to do go from city to city purging any armies or enemies until there are none of us left and we're all dead!"

The dark room began to fill with a golden light from Zadok's amulet and eyes. He dropped the weapon he was carrying and pulled out a naginata Japanese spear staff.

"Zadok I know how much everyone had lost on this journey and how much more we will lose. Some of us could die, we've been over this hundreds of times we are two sides of the same coin. We have to do this because we have the abilities and powers others can't and besides it's our fault, it's my fault!"

The room grew quiet again, as we stared out the windows and holes in the wall. The clicking and scurrying of insect feet on the pavement below once again echoing through the darkness.

"Catalyst we should move now before we need to start taking them out before they take us out." Said Toni. We readied our blades, James, Toni, Agatha and I exited the buildings and hugged the shadows along the buildings until we came across the first group of roaches. I pulled the red sword made from Gabriel's claws out of the homemade sheath tucked it close to my legs. I jumped upon the roaches back and brought the sword into the roaches back and dragged the blade through his head. I pushed my feet down and brought the split roach carcass into the floor and jumped onto the back of the next one. I cut his legs off and crushed the roaches head under my heel.

James has formed his blood sickles and began to rip apart the roaches, tearing wings off, legs off and ripping them in half. Agatha has already started to sand blast the roaches into nothingness when another dozen roach crawled out from the next street. Toni began to blast the roaches with the thermal gun, he grabbed hand full of metal scraps from the floor and loaded them into the chamber at the top of the gun. He fired again and again; the first roach was completely obliterated. Another roach jumped down from a pile of rubble and bit down on Toni's guns cutting it clean in half.

"Agatha shoot your sand at me now!" Toni screamed

"won't that kill you?"

"do it I have a plan!"

Agatha blasted the silica sand at Toni, and he pulled out his thermal pistol and cranked it up to the highest and hottest setting.

Which caused the sand to turn into glass and rip through the roaches hide.

"Catalyst that one's escaping, and we cannot let him return to Annabelle!" Said James

I grabbed a metal sliver knife and threw it into the roaches back, I stuck my hand inside and filled his guts with Asian giant hornet venom. The roach seized up and collapsed dead.

After we killed all the roaches on the street closet to our building we returned to where our friends hid.

"You guys alright in there?" I asked

"Actually, I think you guys better get in here" whispered Zadok.

The others sat bunched tight in a corner of the highest floor. A drone had flown into the window and was broadcasting a message.

"Toni your element of surprise is no more, oh wait it never was, how stupid are you guys. You were on my ship, and then you continued to use my weapons I'm tracking you fools. I simply wanted you to think you were making some sort of ground, celebrating a small victory before so that your defeat would feel all the worse, or better for me. Now surrender or I will be forced to surround your building and kill e one of you. If I don't hear from you in ten minutes, I will assume you chose the latter." Her voice clicked off and the drone began to buzz and hum before it shifted into one of the robotic men. Its hand changed into a gun and he held it toward my chest.

"Nine minutes remaining" Said the robot

"We have to agree that we are not surrendering, I don't know about you,I'll fight until my last breath "Said Willard.

*Whack whack, crack crunch.*A few shards of metal embedded in my cheek as James bashed the robot to pieces. Parts and bits of metal scattered the room. James dropped Willard's war hammer with a loud metallic ring.

"That an answer enough Annabelle, I stand with Catalyst and Willard we'll fight until the last enemy falls or I clot my last ounce of blood."

"You are out of time commencing **attack wave one.**" A second robot blared.

"This is it guys, this will be our last stand, our Alamo a few men against thousands," Said Toni

"Uh wasn't the Alamo a loss though?" Asked James.

"Only from a certain point of view, it bought Sam Austin enough time to rally troops to fight Santa Anna another day and it will buy us enough time to figure out how to get that book and defeat Annabelle." I said

"Enough heroic speeches time to defend or die," Annabelle's voice shouted through one of the drones.

BOOM BOOM BOOM CRACK. A group of the robotic drone man had blasted a hole into the side of the building. Cockroaches and millipedes began to crawl through the hole.

DA DA DA DA DA DA. James has stepped into the center of the room and began blasting through and killing several insects with the thermal Gatling gun. My face was covered in blood and insect goo. My hands tightened on the blade of my sword.

Agatha blasted the flying drones out of the sky one right after the other, until the drone shot metal slivers through her hands.

"AAA what the hell!" Agatha screamed as she fell to the ground and her body collapsed from shock. I swung my sword under hand and sliced through the thick metal covering on the robotic shell. Willard blasted acid and melted the robot from inside out. A solid crossfire had been created between us blasting out the windows and Cardinals, drones, and other bad guys shooting back at us.

I heard the howl of the fermenters outside the building they broke through our defenses and we began to be overrun by the various creatures and men. Everywhere I looked, there were creatures attacking my friends. James was still mowing down the cockroaches and millipedes with the thermal gun until it ran out of chemical energy. He tossed the empty gun into the last roach and crushed him. He formed a long sword and tried to cut down the fermenters. I brought my sword through the arm of a fermenter and the purple blood pooled in the floor.

Willard slammed his war hammer's claw through the drones casing and filled it to the brim with acid.

I slashed my sword through the fermenters again and again attempting to keep them at bay. I stuck my hand in the fermenters open arm and pumped him full of stink ray venom. I launched myself off the mutt's carcass and brought my sword through the next fermenters skull. I was thrown a to the ground and my sword was chewed up and swallowed by a millipede. The insect began to crawl up my legs and seeped its razor-sharp legs deep into my flesh.

I began to pass out and my eyes rolled to the side, I saw Toni smashing and slashing through Cardinals. He brought the battle axe into the back of one and turned to slam it into the next when the Cardinal dropped his sword and grabbed his thermal gun. He pushed the tip of his gun against Toni's chest and pulled the trigger. The heat blast completely incinerated Toni's chest and he fell to the floor life less.

"TONI NO PLEASE, NO NO NO TONI," I screamed. I attempted to blast my way thru the enemies and to Toni's body. My tears were thick and heavy and poured down my face. I fired my thermal pistol through the face of the nearest Cardinal. I pulled the trigger again all I heard was an empty click. I grabbed the soldier's sword coated it in poison as I had a dozen times before.

My knees touched the floors and I pushed my forehead against Toni's. His skin had already started to grow cold.

I felt someone press against my back and I had begun to turn and bring my sword to the man's neck.

"Catalyst it's alright buddy it's me, I'm sorry I'm going to miss him to there is nothing we can do for him now, we have to go get that book or we will never beat her." Said James.

We were able to cut through most of the army when Willard spit acid onto the floor and melted through the fermenter's tough hides. A second wave of drones entered the room and I saw Zadok and Reuben when I could not before.

Reuben was able to turn the air around the drones to a solid and crush the drones before they shift into the robotic soldiers.

"James help Zadok! He's bleeding and weak" Reuben screamed.

The Cardinals began to shoot the acid throwers at our feet, and it melted the floor below us. I dragged Agatha over to where Zadok sat and James coagulated his blood.

The room grew ablaze and enemies grew closer and closer.

"I think it's time we go get that book, instead of keeping her from using it we should figure out how to use it against her," Said Agatha

Agatha and I clasped each other's hands and began to blast the poison coated sand over the Cardinals and the others, it kept them at bay while Reuben placed his hand on the back wall of the building and liquefied the concrete and metal beams. At first it was enough room for each of us to slip through one at a time until Reuben slipped out last.

"Reuben bring down the building on top of those bastards like Sampson did to the philistines."

We ran away from the building as I stared at Toni's body until it was engulfed in flames.

Reuben places both hands into the wall and liquefied enough of the building for the building to collapse. Sending hundreds of pounds of rubble and clouds of soot into the air. The screams of the dozens of soldiers and creatures was muffled as the dust settled.

"let's go guys Toni would want us to grieve when the battle is won." I said.

With the first wave of enemies defeated the street was desolate and quiet. I picked the small bits of metal slivers and shards from the building and my sword.

"I guess since Toni is dead, I will take point, James you get rear, Willard and Agatha right and left flank. Reuben, I know you're not his biggest fan right now, I think you should stay in the center and help Zadok."

Reuben answered with a loud reluctant huff, he wrapped his arm around Zadok's back for support none the less. While we walked toward the United Nations tower, we discussed different ways that Annabelle's powers worked and how we would even get to the top of the tower and get the book.

"Most of our powers, are stemmed from a variation to your blood. Properties in your blood are at extremely heightened levels, James, Catalyst, Willard, even Thermal and slivers powers. My Amulet is locked so that only any member of my family or I may use it. This is possible because when I touch it pricks my finger and in a fraction of a second finds trace genetic markers and DNA. What if we all didn't end up on that planet by accident and even more so what if blood is the key to Annabelle's book. What we can't use the book because we are not her or her kin. We will have to Destroy it and we are going to have to destroy her." Said Zadok.

"Zadok look maybe your right, maybe our entire lives are some great big conspiracy and everything we know is a lie. Maybe we all got our powers from some freaky government test and maybe your right about the Amulet and book being connected. If that were the case though why would they not be able to recreate their experiments and why would they keep us a live and let us meet and especially. Whatever we can figure all this out later the truth is probably in the middle we knew the government was doing it to get rid of us and use the planet as a dumping ground for their cover-ups and experiments anyway you know what right now I really don't care I really do not give a fuck . You're a historian maybe figure it out after we beat Annabelle before we fight the government. I know when it comes down to it, I don't know if I will be able to kill Annabelle.

"Well I understand where your both coming from that whole doomed to repeat history thing and all that, also don't worry if you can't bring yourself to do it, I will kill that psycho bitch myself." Said Agatha

Chapter twenty-five

We finally reached the steps of Annabelle's building when the sun peaked over the horizon and in between the buildings.

"Let's go get that book, for Toni," I said

Zadok threw his spear through the neck of the cardinal guard who guarded the door. Zadok whipped off his blood covered face and the blade of his Naginata. Blast began to come in waves from inside the building.

Agatha blasted tons of thick dense sand from her hands which created a wall so that the thermal blast turned it into glass. We used those few seconds so we could get to cover.

"James do you still have that acid flame thrower. I have an idea. Give the gun to Willard when the tank runs dry, he can refill it," I said.

James pulled the strap off his shoulder and tossed the gun to Willard."

"Behind me! I will douse this side of the building with acid, after the wall is eaten away fire into the building until their firing stops," Willard shouted. The glass wall shattered and popped before melting. I heard the concrete, wood and metal sizzle and bubble before being consumed by the black acid. Only James, Agatha and Reuben still had ammo in their thermal pistols.

The crossfire ensued once again; blast ricocheted off the pavement.

"Ah fuck"! Agatha Yelled and grabbed her shoulder as she caught a blast.

I heard the soldiers and beast inside the building began to scream. First the firing stopped and then the screaming.

"That's it I'm out," Said Zadok. He tossed his empty thermal gun into the entrance way to the building.

One at a time we entered the Unites Nations building. My cheeks were hot and beads of sweat rolled down my forehead and arms. The metal jutted up from the ground twisted, deformed, and still smoking. I saw were dozens of charred Skeletons and mutilated bodies. Those that hadn't died from the direct acid were killed from the smoke inhalation. We looked over the wreckage and picked up the few thermal rounds that had not exploded.

"I think it's time we checked out the rest of the building. Let's get Annabelle and the book." I said.

We searched floor after floor found no trace of Annabelle or anyone.

“Guys something’s not right, the people on the floor are dead I don’t think anyone else is in this building.” Said Agatha.

The hallway flooded with light along with several robotic drones. The drones shifted into robotic soldiers and drew their guns and flame throwers and pressed it into our skulls. The robot that had his gun to my head began to speak. A familiar sweet sadistic voice.

“Really Catalyst maybe I give you guys to much credit. You honestly thought I was going sit at the top of the building waiting for you guys to come attack. the whole lot if you have been mentioning it constantly for two days. Life is not a movie or some crappy book. I was distracting you fools. While you fought my first wave I escaped with the book. Also, if you guys move you will get shot and if you don’t move the robots are rigged to explode.” Said Annabelle. I heard her blow a kiss and click off the radio.

“Honestly, she’s right are we really this damn dum, we expected her to sit and wait at the top of some evil impenetrable tower. We have superpowers why would she not flee,” Screamed Zadok

“Yes, it was foolish, I think we should scold ourselves less and escape more,” I said

We looked at each other and at all the different robotic drones about to kill all of us. There is no way we were going to go out like this. I locked eyes with everyone and nodded.

I slid my hand down my thigh and slid the Cardinal claw knife into my palm.

“Like a clock!” I said

I threw the knife into the robotic drone that was guarding James, James threw a blood knife into the drone on Agatha , Agatha sandblasted the drone on Willard, Willard acid blasted the one on Reuben , Reuben liquefied the drone on Zadok and Zadok threw his spear through the drone that had his gun on me . The drone has fired a blast that singed off a portion of my hair. I rubbed the patch of scalp in disbelief at the near miss.

We all had to push up on our own jaws because we all stared at each other dumb founded by how well that ridicules plan worked.

James formed a blood long sword and cut out the section of windows closest to us.

“Catalyst, Guys look a military convoy. I bet you Annabelle is inside. What do you say we find out?” James asked

“I think I can get us down there fairly,” Said Agatha. She approached the window opening and began to blast sand directly below us until a large ramp like mound of sand formed. One at a time we slid down the sand to the street below.

“Guys wait, what if that’s what she wants, and this is one elaborate plan. I mean think about how easily we escaped those killer drones. They could have as easily shot us all in the heads no problem. Annabelle has been guiding us, controlling us this whole time. We are merely part of the story she controls.” I said

“So, what are you saying we should do nothing, run away?” Agatha asked.

"Exactly, Toni had told me about this battle tactic it's called fake retreat. When they notice we are no longer advancing they will be forced to send a group of soldiers after us. Our small group can certainly move a lot faster than her massive army. She will be forced to send small detachment and when they here we'll kill them. Of course, if anyone else has a better idea I would love to hear it.

I waited for the others to speak up, however even Zadok remained silent.

"That is what we will do then, even from the grave Toni still helps guide us." I said.

We fired several shots in the direction of the convoy before walking in the opposite direction. For a few minutes we made small talk and discussed tactics and who would fight which enemies. Agatha has caught up to where James and I were walking, she nudged my shoulder.

"Catalyst we've gotten pretty lucky this far, I don't know how much longer we have left, and I have to tell you that I forgive you for everything. I know we've been through a lot of stuff and a lot of my friends died in that planet I know some of them were your fault although most weren't and I'm sorry I was mad at you for so long and I hope you can forgive me ."

"Of course, I do Agatha; thank you for Forgiving me I will do whatever I can to watch your back and I know you will watch mine."

We walked for thirty minutes or so and came upon a large Forest in the heart of the city. We stepped upon the grey grass and it crunched under our feet.

"Let's dig in, this is where we will ambush them. Reuben, James you guys dig a fox hole about a mile to the south. The rest of us will pair up and fortify our fighting positions here and up on that hill" I said.

We all picked our defensive positions, forced to dig with our swords and hands. Willard and Zadok chopped down trees to reinforce the Fox hole walls. For e fox hole we created a wooden cover like a wooden bunker.

"Uh Catalyst don't think I'm stupid how big a hole are we supposed to dig? You keep saying fox hole how big is that?

"A Two-man fox hole should be about six feet across and deep enough so that your armpits are above the ground." Zadok Said

"Uh that sounds like it's going to take a while especially if you want to reinforce the walls with the logs. Also, I think the pits supposed to be deep enough to cover your head, then you have a fire step, you can stand on to shoot from," Said Willard

"Well none the less we will never be able to dig a hole of that size with our hands." Said James.

He dragged his jagged stake arm across his forearm and used the blood to create a couple shovels. Willard and Zadok took their position at the top of a large hill.

"Catalyst the soldiers are about three miles out, everyone ready your weapons." Said Zadok

The first few men entered the park. Each wave was made up of Mercenaries, Drones, and Fermenters. We loaded our guns and readied our swords as the men stepped into sight.

"On my count, Now!" I Yelled.

The first few men fell with ease. In order to save ammo, we would take turns firing short burst until they marched no more.

The second wave of Cardinals each had a thermal Gatling gun that completely ate through the logs that covered the fox hole. Zadok pulled a spear out of his amulet and through it into the Thermal gun causing it to explode and create a chain reaction. As usual we were able to hold the men at bay until we began to run low on Ammo.

The thunder of hundreds of feet grew closer, I blast soldier after solider until I caught a thermal blast to the chest. I slipped to the floor and my gun dropped from my hand.

"Catalyst enemies approaching from the south! "Said James.

I tried to stand fell to my knees, my fingers curled around the hilt of my red sword.

"We're being surrounded and were low on ammo," Zadok

Annabelle and her main forces had come upon us. Dozens of Fermenters were about to leap down upon us from above. I finally managed to stand and raised my sword into the air. A cardinal dropped into my fox hole and I blocked his sword with my own. I slid my sword along his and when it fell off, I slit the man in half. The Fermenters began to leap down from one of the hills and attempted to leap into our pit.

Agatha reaches down and placed one hand against the dirt. She began to sand blast the fermenters until only their bones remained. The firing step gave away and she began to sand blast her own face down to the bone. I grabbed her hand and pulled it away from her face. I pulled myself out of the fox hole and Helped Agatha our next. The Cardinals surrounded us, Agatha blasted one in the face and I grabbed the one nearest to me and dragged my sword across his arm until his gun fell out of his hand and into mine. I blasted the man farthest from me and grabbed the arm of the man closest to me. I filled his body with enough poison to kill ten men. I saw James and Reuben fight and destroy an army of robots. Reuben was quick to liquefy any robots James could not rip apart with his blood sickles. Agatha had begun to swallow fermenters and cockroaches with her quicksand.

A larger number of drones began to descend upon us from the sky. The first one blasted Agatha with a giant syringe of yellow ooze. One that I knew too well. The venom of a king cobra.

"Agatha Nooo! Please be ok!" I screamed I sliced through man and beast again and again attempting to reach where she lay.

"James help Agatha please, guys we need to regroup!

"Aa Fuck my back!" James screamed

I saw him sink to the ground with a massive bloody slash to his back.,

I felt a stab to my lower back; I checked the wound with my hand and felt a large amount of blood seep through my fingers I passed out from shock and fell to the ground.

"Wake up my dear,"

I felt thin fingers slide down my face they passed through my deep scars and stop under my chin.

"Catalyst because I love you, I thought I'd give you one last chance to join me. You are surrounded and unimaginably out numbered. I could have you all killed right now with one command. Now I ask you one last time. Join me or you will all die right here and now." Said Annabelle.

They had me strapped to a downed tree, James, Agatha, and Reuben laid at my feet bloody and motionless. The book was tightly wrapped in Annabelle's arms.

"Annabelle you should know by now I will

Not give up and I certainly not help you take over the world and kill thousands of people. Now give me the book or they will drop you where you stand."

"Who is going to drop me where I stand, the babbling coward old man or the flight less dragon?" Said Annabelle

"Director Bishop the old man escaped he is dripping blood, however we did slay the dragon." Said David.

They dropped a black and purple carcass at my feet. A red sword had been snapped off after going through his heart. Tears began to pool in my eyes before slowly sliding down my cheeks. He was barely recognizable, I knew it was Willard.

The tears came quicker they became thick and heavy.

"Why, No Willard I'm sorry, I'm so sorry it's my fault it's all my fault!" I screamed

"Dude shut the hell up he's dead, all of your friends are dead and your right it is your fault," Said David.

The man cut off Willard's claw and began to drag it across my shoulder blades and through the knife wounds from before.

"Aaaa Fuck you, I'm going to fucking kill you!"

I felt the pain in e inch of my body. As I screamed blood and spit seeped from my mouth

"Catalyst your right I know you will never stop until you have my book and I'm dead or captured so I know that I have to do what you said to everyone else I have to let him kill you before you can kill me"

She gave me one last peck on the cheek, and she walked away us of site of my being tortured.

David pulled his arm back getting ready drive the claw into my shoulder again. I saw his hand release and the talon hit the floor. An Egyptian dagger had been thrown through his hand and blood seeped from his palm.

"Ack what the fuck, get him! said David.

He pulled the dagger out of his hands and dropped it at his feet.

"Zadok watch out!"

He reached into his amulet and pulled out a thick shield. He shoved the shield into the chest of the men in front of him which knocked them to the floor. Zadok dug the xiphos sword deep into a Cardinals shoulder. The Fermenters closed in and began to circle Zadok, paused and readied to pounce. He held the sword above his head ready to bring it down into the fermenter's skull. He swung the blade downward before it could make contact, he collapsed exhausted and drained from overuse of the amulet.

Annabelle returned to where I was, I was chained to the tree. She pulled David's knife out of my back and handed it back to him.

"Lieutenant restrain the old man and bring me a prison transport craft." Said Annabelle

"If you really loved my Annabelle let me know one thing before you kill me. How does your book work?"

She pulled out the book and flipped to a new page. After she wrote a few paragraphs she dragged her finger across the blade of the Egyptian dagger and sealed the page with a blood seal.

Out of the corner of my eye I saw Reuben's chest lift off the ground.

"Reuben it's not too late we can still win, take the ring do the same trick you did at Niagara Falls!" Said Zadok.

He tossed the ring through the air and Reuben caught it in his cupped hands as he stood.

"Reuben do it now! liquefy the ground and trap them!"

"I'm afraid that's not going to happen Catalyst, Reuben works with me. I will say thank you for giving us the power enhancing ring which was the last thing we needed from you and now we have no reason to keep you alive." Said Annabelle

David dropped Zadok's bloody body at my feet, tears swelled in my eyes.

"What's should we do with his amulet and who do we kill first?

Reuben walked over and ripped the Amulet off Zadok's chest. I saw the light dim in Zadok's eyes, and he passed out

"Kill them all I don't care what order, however, kill Catalyst last so that he has to watch his friends die." Said Reuben

"Reuben how could you do this, why would you do this. You're a good guy, you fought besides us for nearly a year why would you side with Annabelle. How could you order the death of your friends?" I asked

"Catalyst the problem with you is you think so simple minded. You think People are good or bad friend or foe. That if people are your friends, they have this undying loyalty to you. Well guess what we were never friends. You kept me alive and got me back to Earth.

You always argued with me belittled me tried to suppress my power. You took the ring away and scolded me for Saving your life. Well you know what you taught me that I should look out for myself and kill people before they can kill you. You were too dumb to listen to the fact that this is a battle and the government is bringing a war. When they do, I will stand more powerful then everyone here. I will have all your powers and more. I will take over the world and I will use your powers to do it."

Reuben placed a piece of tape over my mouth and began to drag a blade across Zadok's throat.

"Catalyst I'm sorry this is the way it must be all we want to do is save the world and bring peace and if we have to rule it to do it then we will." Said Annabelle.

All hope was lost. I felt truly and utterly defeated, I had hoped Annabelle could be turned she had Willard and Toni killed, James and Agatha are already dead or close to it. That could have been it I could have let them win and finally end my fighting. No, I could not have let Zadok die knowing it was my fault for wanting to fight until that last breath when he wanted to flee months ago. The problem with fighting until the last breath is that you must die. I saw them about to kill Zadok and I would not let anyone take anyone from me ever again. No matter what I had to do I would win I would save my friends and defeat the bad guys.

I dragged my mouth across my chest again and again until the tape tore. I scooted forward and cut the rope using the dagger.

Actions faster than reaction. I reached into my shirt and pulled out the necklace of talons. I leaned forward and jammed the talons deep into Reuben's chest. Before the soldiers could attack and grabbed his ring and slipped it onto my finger. The green band flashed, and I felt the metal pins push into my skin.

I pumped Inland Taipan venom into the air until the body hit the floor. The few robots that remained I Slashed with David's red sword. I turned around and the thousands of bodies remained motion less. The ring had given me the ability to emit my venom in the form of a gas yet creating such a toxic dose on a grand scale was still enough to drain my energy and I was forced to sleep.

Chapter twenty-six

When I awoke, I walked the battlefield searching for my friends or anyone who might have survived my wave of poison. I had killed so many people, I would not be betrayed again I was tired of being betrayed and tired of watching my friends die I did what I had to do to save them. Thousands of bodies piled on top of one another it took me a long time to find my friends.

I kneeled when I got to Annabelle's body and I placed my hand above her mouth and filled her nostrils with an anti-venom gas. Before she could awake, I tied her to the same tree she had tied me to.

One at a time I found and brought over all my friends, James, Agatha, Zadok and Willard's dead body. After I brought each one back, I gave them the anti-venom and watched to see if it would take and if they'd get better.

"hush what the hell happened" James muttered. Hey, awoke and sat up.

"Reuben revealed himself and basically said we turned him evil because we were mean to him or some bullshit about wanting power and self-preservation, so I stabbed him in the chest and killed the entire army with snake venom." I said

James looks around dumbfounded and shocked. He slid his hand down the slash mark in his back that had hardened over.

"Hey Catalyst, thank you for saving my life," Said Zadok

"Someone had to save your scrawny old neck, honestly though as much as we fight, I love you man and I will always have your back."

"Even though you're a total dumbass sometimes I will always have your back too. Of course, it's because you're a dumbass that I will have to watch your back."

James and Zadok were able to stand after several minutes and the covered Willard with their coats.

Why was Agatha still not waking up I have her the anti-venom. I gave her CPR and violently pushed my weight into her as her chest popped and crunches. Then I remembered she has been taken down by Cobra venom first. I slit her arm and pressed my fingers into her wound and gave her a dose of the cobra anti-venom.

"Catalyst? We won, we won. I can't believe we were able to stop them." Said Agatha

She bolted to her feet and jumped into my arms hugging me tight.

"Catalyst how did we win? Where is Reuben, what happened to the book and what the hell is she doing here." Said Agatha

She dropped to the floor and sand blasted Annabelle's restraints off.

"Catalysts I thought we decided we would kill her, kill her before she could kill us. My promise still stands I will kill her. What do you think she can be redeemed she is a villain? Even if she wakes up, she will only pretend to be good again to save her life. Well guess what this is not some stupid movie, you don't get to kill thousands of people and then turn around and apologize and rejoin the group like nothing happened."

Agatha took a few steps closer to where Annabelle laid.

"I said if we had to, we don't, the book is missing, and I think enough people died today don't you think. Besides you would kill an unarmed woman." I said.

"Agatha you know Catalyst is right, that's not you we can't kill people like that, or we are as big a monster as her." Said James.

James began to pull Agatha away from where Annabelle was laying and pushed her in front of me.

"Well don't look at me I'm not going to stop you, she captured us, bled us, tortured us and tried to kill us. I have no problem If you kill her," Said Zadok

"Catalyst you can't claim to be good, you killed several thousand men in one breath you are not innocent, and I am a monster."

The sand below our feet began to shift and move.

"No Agatha don't do it, please I still love her!" I screamed.

James and I tried to hold her back, we could not stop her. The sand below Annabelle began to move and bounce. The ground transformed into quicksand and then swallowed Annabelle without a trace.

I clawed at the dirt until I was up to my elbows, I'm soot, and tears had begun to stream down my face.

"Agatha how could you do that…"

"Catalyst she hadn't awoken anyway there was a good chance she was probably already dead" Said Zadok.

"So, Guys what do we do now? For the first time in years we don't have anything to escape from no one to fight. We finally won." Said James

I looked across at all the dead soldiers, all the guns and swords.

"I'm afraid not James, we may have won a single battle. Let us not forget about the President and his global army. This was one battle with one group of people who wanted power we are going to have to fight thousands. Especially the president who undoubtedly new of this fight. He probably was hoping we would all destroy ourselves. For now, I say we stay in the city, collect weapons and ammo, if we have any hope of taking on the president's forces, we are going to need more people to join our team."

For all the trouble we went through to get to the city, and the fact that Annabelle's forces had killed any UN and troops and presidential forces. That meant that New York was the only free city in the world and the four of us vowed to keep it that way. We made the city our base and our home. In the center of the city we buried Willard and Toni and dedicated monuments to everyone else we had lost.

For the longest time I didn't speak to Agatha, I couldn't even look her in the eyes. Once I realized if it had been anyone Annabelle, I would have done the same thing. We made up, and the four of us began to train e day, we collected as many weapons as we could find. Spent months working on a base and going from building to building and picked out anything we could use to help us with our cause.

After four months had passed, we had completely sealed off the city with concrete wall 12 feet high. Each of us laid claim to a building that we tweaked and made our own. Life was good for now.

One Morning I heard Zadok screaming into the steps of the United Nations building.

"Hey Zadok man what's going on, you need to calm down. Remember you're in a weaker state without your amulet. Now what's going on" I said.

"That's exactly its Catalyst. No matter what you, James and Agatha will always have weapons at your disposal, I won't. I am weaker than ever. The way is coming, and I will have no chance." Said Zadok

I saw he fury and sadness in his eyes. His arms flailing about.

"Zadok you are one of the fiercest warriors I have ever had the honor of fighting beside. We will find your Amulet or if we have to a new weapon or power to call your own. Also, we don't have to rush into battle right away, we've been fighting for our lives for a solid year straight. I say we learn to relax for a while. Take it easy maybe find some good food and some nice places to sleep. See what this living life is all about"

The End

Epilogue

Plink, Plink, plink. The blood fell into the beaker one drop at a time. The dark laboratory flickered to life with glowing lights, colorful test tubes and experiments lined the walls. Several bodies hung from hooks as blood drained from their bodies.

"Reuben did you retrieve all of the bodies like I asked you too. We will need e drop of Ms. Bishop's blood if we have any hopes of using her book," I said.

"Yes, Colonel Collins after I awoke, I dug up Annabelle, Toni, Willard and the others like you asked. The professor said there is still enough blood to utilize its capabilities."

Broken and dismembered robot parts scattered the laboratory tables and spilled onto the floor.

"You not only failed to retrieve the ring of ultimate potential, you let Catalyst take it. The president will not be happy."

"Listen I don't want to hear any of that, I not only survived being stabbed and poisoned. I was able to liquefy the blade and solidify it fast enough to appear that I had been stabbed. They all destroyed each other. I was able to get the book, the blood and this." Said Reuben

He pulled out Zadok's amulet and placed in onto

The table with a loud clank.

"Colonel with this amulet we can have any weapon we ever wanted, and if we can crack it perhaps, we can get another ring."

"I was under the assumption we would need his blood to activate the amulet."

"We have it, during the Central Park battle my blade grazed his throat. Each activation only requires a drop of blood. We have a vial."

"Excellent we have everything we need then, it's time for the next battle to begin. Take the upgraded robotic drones, UN troops and whatever supplies you need. I will keep the book and you can have the amulet. Go retake New York City, crush the uprising before it can come to fruition and bring the President Catalyst's severed head.

Made in the USA
Las Vegas, NV
22 July 2021